Dark Orchid

Dark Orchid

Michael J. Shanks

Winchester, UK
Washington, USA

First published by Roundfire Books, 2013
Roundfire Books is an imprint of John Hunt Publishing Ltd., Laurel House, Station Approach,
Alresford, Hants, SO24 9JH, UK
office1@jhpbooks.net
www.johnhuntpublishing.com
www.roundfire-books.com

For distributor details and how to order please visit the 'Ordering' section on our website.

Text copyright: Michael J. Shanks 2012

ISBN: 978 1 78099 992 0

A CIP catalogue record for this book is available from the British Library.

Design: Stuart Davies

Printed and bound by CPI Group (UK) Ltd, Croydon, CR0 4YY

We operate a distinctive and ethical publishing philosophy in all
areas of our business, from our global network of authors to
production and worldwide distribution.

Acknowledgements

The list of people I should thank for tolerating me is almost endless so I will skip them and thank them at some later point, probably.

For help with this book I would like to thank Allan Davidson, Nikki Mackay, Jen and my parents for their advice, proof reading and not laughing at me when I said I was going to write it in the first place.

Finally, thanks to Cameron for enthusiastically joining in with my sham multi-tasking. You survived so no harm done.

Prologue

He opened one eye. His other eye was stuck shut for reasons unknown to him. He could taste blood, acid bile and smooth waxy leather from something shoved in his mouth. His body ached horribly. He had no concept of how long he had been there nor how he had got there. With his one eye he glanced around but couldn't make anything out. Nothing in focus. Nothing familiar. Nothing at all. Darkness and a fairy light shimmer of white filled his limited, blurred vision. It took a while but eventually the realisation that he was incredibly cold registered and this kick-started the signals rushing through his body. His brain caught up and his body screamed at him as he flexed his legs and arms, trying to move. Bindings; rope and tape, held him firm and dug deep into his skin. He could feel everything but nothing. Numbness blanketed his body. He could feel pain but not what caused it. It felt like the skin had been stripped from his body. Nerves exposed and raw.

He couldn't look down but he knew he was naked.

His body started to act on its own, disconnected from his brain. Control mechanisms took over and started shutting down, compartmentalising and sacrificing for the greater good. He wasn't aware enough to panic but his heart pumped double time hard inside his chest regardless. Like a circling of the wagons it was retreating. Warm blood pumped through his central core and nowhere else. The extremities were already lost and his body knew this, even if he didn't. He shook his head side to side but could only move a tiny amount. Masking tape held his head tight against what felt like rough tree bark. His breathing was laboured through blood-clogged nostrils.

He stood still.

Tied tight to a pine tree.

Not shivering. Not moving.

Just breathing and waiting.

* * *

James Bisset thanked the driver and stepped off the number 54 bus. He hunched himself up against the weather and walked fast down the street towards his flat. It was early evening but he was alone. Tonight wasn't a night for hanging around. Normally at this time of the day the narrow tenement and tree-lined street would be filled with children playing. Eking out every minute of daytime before their tea was called and the day ended. Tonight the weather had washed them all away. It was deserted. Arriving at his flat he quickly keyed in the security code and stepped into the relative comfort of the shared close. There was a damp feel to the air. It smelled musty as the three-day rain storm worked its way through the seals on the exterior door. The mail inside his mailbox was curled at the edges. He could feel dampness on the paper. Two flights up, he counted the stairs as he always did to confirm what he already knew; 1, 2, 3, 4, 5, 6, turn, 1, 2, 3, 4, 5, 6 turn, 2 steps and he was standing outside his flat, 1/3 23 Morningside Brae.

The new lock turned smoothly and he stepped into the warm, carpeted, dry interior leaving his shoes outside on the welcome mat.

As Edinburgh flats go James's was at the very comfortable end of the scale. Two bedrooms. 120sq ft. A refurbished tenement flat in an upscale suburb of Edinburgh. Fifteen-minute bus journey to the city centre. He had purchased it two years ago and still enjoyed the silence inside as he closed the new door and padded around in his socks. It was his, he shared it with no one. It was styled as he liked and furnished as he wanted. Decorated plainly and sparsely, white and cream walls, light brown carpet throughout. No fuss or clutter. Visitors would sometimes comment that it was lacking a feminine touch. He would just shrug and point out he was a guy. He didn't care. It was his and he loved closing the door on the world, loosening his tie and being himself, in his place. The only exception to the overall theme was Lindsey and Rose's room. They had decorated it together one weekend when they were staying with him and the result was a riotous explosion of colour, dinosaurs and stickers. He kept the door shut when they weren't there. He didn't like being reminded of their absence nor the clutter contained within. On drop off Sunday as Lindsey called it he would return to the flat, walk around the room tidying up. Throwing toys into baskets, closing drawers, stripping the bunk beds and then closing the door.

They left a void which he preferred to keep contained within that room.

Pulling a bottle of beer from the fridge, he noticed a bill from Joanna, his cleaning lady, standing against his telephone answering machine. It was evident she had been today. James kept everything immaculate but he still preferred to have someone come, once every two weeks to make sure. Joanna had even told him she wasn't needed but he had insisted. He smiled at the neatly placed magazines and just knew that there wouldn't be a speck of dust to be found in the flat. A proud Polish woman, she was determined to earn her money. He placed the bill on top of the damp unopened mail and then clicked play on his answer phone. It was flashing a digital number two.

The first message, double-glazing. He could faintly hear the familiar noise of call-centre hubbub in the background behind Andy, the salesman's pitch. Andy had an Indian accent. He pressed delete. 'Second message,' the robot voice announced.

'James! Answer your fuckin mobile!' Ewan's voice shouted out of the machine at him. 'Call me for fuckssake. You read your email? Oh Christ. James FUCKIN PICK UP YOUR PHONE.'

He stood there, beer bottle in hand staring at the phone. Ewan's voice was panicked and loaded with anxiety. No more messages the robot voice confirmed. It clicked and was silent.

He stood there for a full two seconds staring at the machine before doing anything.

He then pulled his laptop from his bag switching it on as he did so whilst simultaneously grabbing his mobile phone. Shit, seven missed calls, all from Ewan. His phone was on silent due to him being in a meeting all afternoon and he had forgotten to change it back. He hit call back and sat at the breakfast bar waiting for his laptop to cycle through its power up process.

The call went straight to voice mail.

'Ewan, James. Got your message. Call me.'

He pressed the red button on the phone and keyed in his password on the laptop. As it finalised its power up he carried it through to the office desk in the bay window of his living room. He took a mouthful of beer as he walked across the long thick-carpeted living room in his socks. Once sat in the leather office chair he clicked on the email icon.

As the unread emails started filling the screen two stood out. One from Ewan re: Merry Christmas and the original message further down the screen.

He double clicked this and the message filled the screen.

SnataClaws34#27@gmail.com was the sender. Subject 'Merry Christmas'. No text, just a Video file attachment.

James double clicked the file and waited as the appropriate program started up.

His screen turned to black.

He clicked the play button.

As the video started to play the wind buffeted the bay window in front of him. The glass rocked and the rain hit the window like gravel. He never even heard it.

* * *

Footsteps in frozen snow make a cracking sound. Very distinct, and in a snow-muffled environment also very loud. Each footstep is a test as you move your body weight from one foot to the other. The frozen layer on top either holds or cracks. Snowshoes are designed to spread the weight and thus avoid the foot plunging down into the snow. A few steps in deep snow without snowshoes is physically exhausting and also very noisy. It would be very difficult, if not impossible, to creep up on someone at night in frozen snow.

Fortunately, though, tonight stealth wasn't required and in any case the sound was lost. Drowned out by the wheezing and cursing Galston McGee made as he trudged, slipped and crawled his way up the hill. His beard was white with frost. His ill-fitting, cheap, ski clothes sounded like he was wearing an outfit made from heavy-duty plastic bags. Without snow shoes he slowly dragged himself and the rucksack of equipment up the hill from the snow covered road. With every exhausting step he cursed his boss. He cursed this country. He cursed his forty-five years of smoking but most of all he cursed the fucking little Fenian cunt up ahead. In his mind he had already decided he was the reason he was here having to act out this over-dramatic pantomime. Why no just dae him the now, tonight, here? He had asked a few weeks ago. Sandy was determined though to make a show of it, 'tae put the fear o God inna them anyplace we fuckin want.' He glared at him and that was that. Galston booked the tickets that afternoon.

Over the years Galston had done a lot of people. Mostly using whatever was closest to hand. Half a brick. A bin lid. A knife. In an alley or a bus stop somewhere, anywhere. Depressingly fitting places. Bleeding out amongst the fag butts and piss puddles or behind a wheelie-bin stinking of week old rotting pakora. Sometimes he was instructed to do it with a specific weapon or burn the body or take something. A wallet. A finger. It really depended on the circumstances. He never questioned the reasoning behind it, just did as he was told. This kept his life as he liked it, simple. This group were different though. They had really gotten to Sandy. They were smart and young, the sort who had been fed a diet of *Lock Stock and Two Smoking Barrels* where the gangsters were smiling, caricatures of the real world. They had directly rebuffed his approaches with threats of their own. This, just in itself, wasn't an unusual occurrence given their chosen line of work. But for Sandy for some reason this was different and they had somehow managed to do something Galston rarely saw. They had managed to really fucking piss him off.

* * *

The day Craig died was a bad day. A bad day for everyone, but, as James had just found out, a very bad one for Craig. Susan, his wife had taken it hard. Especially the way it happened. Three weeks ago his belongings and car were found abandoned in a South Queensferry car park. This came shortly after the sighting of a man standing on the bridge had sparked an alert and realistically left little doubt in anyone's mind. There was no message or note. Just the car containing the usual in-car debris, his wallet and a picture of Susan and the kids on the passenger seat. Later that day James had spoken with the police and had given them almost all the information he knew. Yes, he seemed happy. No, no reason for this. No pressure at work beyond the normal. No he wasn't a drug user. Alcohol? No more than the normal and it went on. The police left after an hour having completed a required step. Their investigation was already closed barring the paperwork.

James sat staring at his laptop computer screen silently.

He had just witnessed the truth about Craig and it was a long way from taking a suicidal header off the Forth Road Bridge. He watched the grainy video and half-expected it to be a joke. The balaclava man on the screen to suddenly fall over or slip. A *Candid Camera* moment. He willed someone grinning like a mad man to jump out behind him and point at the camera hidden in a lamp or TV. He would laugh and say something which would eventually be beeped out.

No one jumped out though and there wasn't a hidden camera. This was real. It *had* happened and he just sat there watching it play out slowly on his laptop. A voice clearly and calmly explained if he didn't from that very moment toe the fucking line and do exactly what they wanted, Ewan would be next, then Sarah. If necessary they would then move onto the kids. A heavy chill ran through him as they were mentioned by name.

'Eventually, you had better fuckin believe me, you *will* dae this,' the heavily accented voice told him.

* * *

As Galston approached the trees he saw the man and smiled. The darkness had already descended over him. He was as he had left him; naked and tied to a tree with cheap blue plastic rope and masking tape. Steam was rising from his head and his breathing was laboured through blood-clogged nostrils. The snow at his feet had melted away. His body looked ghostly white against the dark Alpine backdrop. It was -15c.

This is the real world you stupid fucker. No trendy music and no slapstick comedy bad guys. We're real and this is *really* going to hurt. Galston thought he might even start to enjoy himself. He dumped the gear with relief, stretched out his aching shoulders and clicked the muscles in his neck. As he started unpacking the video camera, the tripod and the rest of equipment he began to explain to his prisoner what he was going to do. In detail. It took him a while to setup. A mixture of thick gloves and a lifetime of avoiding hi-tech meant it took him more than fifteen minutes to get everything ready. Eventually he was ready and as the green light blinked, he reached into the rucksack to take out the last two items. A small handheld axe and a hacksaw.

The man struggled against the bindings. Most of his strength had already left his frozen body and every feeble movement only served to tighten the frozen ropes. Galston smiled and winked at him before pulling a balaclava over his face and stepping in front of the camera into a ghostly pool of light.

He carried the hacksaw under his arm. The axe hung limply at his side.

Craig stared wildly as he approached and desperately tried to move. He tried to do something, anything. He tried to speak, to plead with the man, but the leather glove shoved in his mouth started to work its way down his throat as he gasped. He was choking. He gagged and frothy saliva foamed around the remaining piece sticking out.

Galston ignored him and without hesitation crouched down and swung the axe hard against his bare ankle. Bone shattered under the impact. Skin ripped open. He pulled the axe back and for the briefest of moments saw pink bone marrow and white flesh before dark red blood filled the wound and poured down the ankle like a dam breached. Craig screamed but no sound came out. His body jerked and convulsed against the bindings. Thousands of tiny ice crystals, shaken from the tree, fell softly to earth. They glistened magically in the bright light of the camera.

Galston swung the axe harder the second time, he was aiming for the centre of the open wound. He missed and the axe stuck deep into freezing bone an inch above. Cursing he pulled it out and swung a third time. This time it cracked through what was left of the anklebone and dug into the calf muscle behind. It was stuck in what felt like rubber and he had to work the blade out side to side to remove it. Reaching down he picked up the hacksaw and quickly sawed through the remaining muscle. The foot fell to the snow and blood-covered forest floor with a dull thump. Blood flowed freely from the stump and melted the snow below. Grass and pine needles were clearly visible mixed with the steaming red liquid and the severed foot.

Galston stood up breathless and kicked it out of the way. He dropped the bloody saw and looked closely into Craig's bruised and swollen face. It was barely recognisable as the young man he had walked down the forest path with less than an hour ago, screwed up and contorted as it was with pain.

Galston showed no emotion and turned around, picked up the axe and swung it again. This time he aimed just below the knee. His swing was a lot harder this time.

Craig swallowed half of the glove and lost consciousness.

* * *

James clicked pause on the laptop and leaned back into his seat. The last seconds of Craig's life were frozen on the screen in front of him. Having watched it through once he now knew what was coming and didn't need or want to put himself through that again. He just sat there and looked at Craig, his best friend, a few seconds before he died.

This was now three weeks after it had happened. He had genuinely cried with grief as he hugged Susan at the bodiless funeral. His best friend had taken his own life and he was at a loss as to why. Now, any grief he might have had was utterly lost in fear and panic. He just sat there staring at the screen. He was acutely aware of the noises around him, his world condensed down to that time, that place. The cars passing outside. The wind and rain against his windows. The quiet ticking of his desk clock. His mobile phone ringing.

His heart was pounding inside his ribcage. He could feel his shirt move in time with the beat. A metallic taste filled his mouth. His lips tingled and his brain worked on overdrive as he tried to figure out what to do.

What to do to make sure the same thing didn't happen to him.

Chapter 1

The radio alarm was as old as its owner, and as the black paper Rolodex display flipped over from 6.59 to 7.00am it burst into life.

The dark room was instantly filled with news and static, white noise and an unintelligible mix of jingles and voices. It served its purpose and James wearily climbed out of bed, padding naked in its direction. It was purposely placed away from the bed on the window ledge, the other side of the room. He stood for a second stretching in front of it before turning the volume down. The urge to turn it off and climb back under the duvet was close to irresistible but he knew he couldn't that morning. Instead he glanced out the window to the dark street outside. It was very dark, middle of the night dark, and for a very brief moment he thought he might have set the alarm wrong or it was simply not working but as he stood there he saw some signs of life. A car passed by and in the tenement building opposite there were some lights on. He checked his watch, 7.02am.

He walked through to the kitchen, clicked the switch on the coffee machine and then headed for the bathroom. Standing in front of the mirror he studied his stubbly face. He was tired but then after only four hours of sleep he couldn't expect anything else. Apart from his current bed-creased weariness he was relatively content with his appearance. After thirty-eight years his body was still holding up reasonably well. His slim physique had filled out a little since his early twenties but not to the extent he even really noticed or cared. The only real signs of age were the flecks of grey peppering his short dark hair and a few lines on his face. Everyone gets older he thought to himself idly as he lathered shaving foam over the stubble and started his morning routine. Twenty minutes later he was sat drinking the coffee in his kitchen. A small TV showed Sky News as he scrolled through his emails on his laptop. Nothing interesting but he still scanned through, accepting meeting requests and deleting the rubbish.

His mobile phone started ringing. It was Craig.

'Morning!' Craig was his usual cheery self. 'Ready?'

'Aye, when you here?'

'Ten minutes, see you outside.' Craig hung up. James placed the phone back on the counter and continued scanning the overnight emails before powering the laptop down, double checking his bag and switching the electricity off in his flat. Fifteen minutes later they were working their way out of the city, flowing easily in the opposite direction to the rush hour traffic as they headed towards the airport.

Edinburgh airport is located eight miles west of the city. Close to the Firth of Forth and its famous bridges, it's windswept and clearly has ambitions well above its station. It proudly claims everywhere you care to look to be an international contender but the reality is only just. The bulk of the volume passing through its halls are domestic. Small propeller planes hop north to Inverness or west to the islands carrying mail and a few passengers. The larger jets sit waiting to fly their passengers south to one of London's many airports or Manchester for transfers. Daily there are a few direct international flights to European destinations and in the summer months charter flights fly holiday makers further afield to the Spanish Balearics or some other sunny holiday destination. In comparison to its European peers it's a small pretender and it looks that way.

The overall appearance of the airport is one of an out of season holiday resort. A bit worn, a bit threadbare and in need of a good clean.

Craig parked his car in the short-term car park and they walked towards the garish yellow terminal building.

Ewan was waiting for them outside. Standing alongside a group of smokers sucking up industrial quantities of nicotine to last them their journey. He was dressed similar to both James and Craig with a dark overcoat on top of his dark suit. His large frame and dress gave him an imposing air. He stood waiting next to a black and silver trolley bag looking decidedly out of place next to the huddled smokers and the worn terminal.

James and Craig both nodded at him as they approached and he fell into line as they walked three abreast into the departures hall. They had already checked in and were travelling hand luggage only so within five minutes were sat in the relative quiet of the BMI business lounge opening up their laptops.

'It go through?' James asked Craig as he clicked keys.

'Hang on would you?'

James was impatient, always had been. Christmas night was always a sleepless one for him as a child and when Lyndsey, his first child, was overdue it drove him insane. Patience and downtime weren't happy bedfellows within his psychological makeup.

He got up to join Ewan at the coffee machine and made two, one for himself and one for Craig. The lounge was quiet. Apart from the three of them there was only one other occupant, a young man reading a newspaper.

'There you go,' Craig said, pointing at the screen as James took the seat next to him.

James followed his finger tracing down a long list of numbers, each one had no indication where they were from but the dates and the values were sufficient proof.

'You sure?' he asked.

'Look,' Craig said pointing at the top of the screen. 'First is always £20,000 aye? With early payment discount that's the £19,000 there,' he tapped his finger on the first number in the left hand column. He seemed a little irritated he had been questioned at all. 'What else would it be?'

'Ok.'

'Tell me about last night? What happened?' Craig asked him.

'What happened last night?' Ewan asked both of them sitting down on the opposite seat.

'Jee-mac here,' Craig started patting James's knee, 'had a hot date last night, didn't you?' he said sarcastically.

'Really? You?' Ewan said picking up a newspaper. 'Nice personality?'

'Fuck off would you,' James responded, then continued. 'No, horrible. Nice tits though.'

Ewan smiled at this. Craig turned the screen on his laptop to face both of them.

'It worked guys,' he said grinning widely and patting his fingers over the numbers on the screen. Craig always the optimist sat holding the laptop. For Craig it was a logical thing, he plans it and mostly Ewan and James execute it. This was their division of labour and it was working. Never any thought to what happens if it doesn't work. Of course it will work, why wouldn't it? Positive things happen to positive people would have been his mantra had he felt the need for one. He didn't though, things never went wrong for Craig so why would he need to work at it?

James smiled and nodded. Ewan looked over and then continued reading his newspaper largely unimpressed that they had just managed to successfully overcome the checks, controls and balances of a FTSE100 company. £19,000 had just been transferred to their holding account and would be followed by many more. The first transfer was the litmus test, once it was through the rest would be relatively easy.

This was their fifth company.

Craig turned the laptop around again and the room fell quiet. James sat there sipping his coffee. Ewan munched on a shortbread finger supplementing the gap between breakfast and his morning snack. He read the sports pages and Craig clicked away on his laptop, moving the funds quickly and assuredly, exactly as James had shown him. Leaving no trace as they waited for the flight to Zurich to be called. Ewan glanced up at the television monitor.

'So tell me about her?' he asked James.

'Like I said. Shit personality, nice tits.'

Their flight was called.

It was particularly violent turbulence which woke James up some time later. He had dozed off as they taxied and snored his way through take-off. Ewan was sat beside him shifting uncomfortably in his seat.

'Statistically speaking...' he started.

'I fucking know OK.' Ewan interrupted him a little too loudly. Some of the other passengers looked around disapprovingly.

'I fucking know the statistics,' he continued in a hushed voice, 'but stats mean nothing when you are six miles up.' Ewan gripped the armrests as he spoke.

Ewan was of a nervous disposition. James and Craig had thought long and hard about bringing him in in the first place. It wasn't a trust thing, they trusted him. It was more a confidence thing. Would he be able to perform under pressure? This was the question and over the last two years he had categorically proved them wrong. Ewan's nervousness seemed to be restricted to only certain things, flying, girls, public speaking, conflict, to name just a few James was aware of. When it came to defrauding a company out of millions Ewan was the ultimate iceman, cool as you like. Whilst Craig and James were sweating, Ewan was calm and confident. Proof, if any were needed, he thought slouching in his seat that the brain is about as rational as Daffy Duck.

James smiled sleepily at this as he watched Ewan staring out the window watching the wing wobble. The seatbelt sign came on with a bing, the plane rolled and bumped violently again and he fell back to sleep leaving Ewan alone with his irrational terror.

An hour later and much to Ewan's relief they landed smoothly. The aircraft taxied to the modern glass and steel terminal building and with the usual Swiss efficiency they were collecting their bags from the carousel as soon as they had arrived there.

'You gotta love the Swiss eh?' Ewan said, much more relaxed

now as they walked towards the green 'nothing to declare' door at customs. They nodded at the customs officials and entered Switzerland proper.

A short but expensive taxi ride took them to their hotel. The air temperature was -6c with bright sunshine, a perfectly clear January day.

The Drei Schwan Hotel is located in the old town of Zurich, on the southern bank of the Limmat river. It's situated close enough to the business heart of the city to charge a premium and just far enough away to charge a little bit more. The building it occupies has been a hotel in some shape or form for over 500 years but it only became the Three Swans recently after significant investment. It is a small private boutique hotel, offering thirty rooms. Modern, quiet and discreet. It is very popular with the super-rich, the rich and the sort of people who value anonymity over price.

They pulled up outside and as Craig settled the fare James and Ewan headed straight to the reception. Inside they were welcomed back by name. They had stayed in this hotel many times but whether they were recognised or the reception team had been briefed in advance was a moot point. They took pride in the small things in this hotel and they knew it was the doing it that counted, not how they did it. James smiled pleasantly at the receptionist as she checked him in while two other hotel staff dealt with Craig and Ewan with a similar absence of fuss.

That evening, after dinner, they sat drinking in the hotel bar. The fire was roaring and giving off enough heat to warm a room three times larger than the small bar they occupied.

'Think they are serious?' Ewan said to no one in particular. Over dinner they had skirted the subject, talking about anything and everything but. It was Ewan who blinked first.

'The threats?' Craig said turning to him and then shaking his head he continued without waiting for an answer. 'Naw doubt it, I've never heard of them and I'm sure Tony has sorted it. Minor players. I'm more concerned how they found out.'

James sat staring at the fire. 'It could be really serious you know?'

'Not a lot we can do about it though is there?' Craig said directly to him. This topic had been discussed too much and they needed to move on.

Craig was the leader. No one said it, no one acknowledged it outright but they all knew if there was an official hierarchy then Craig would be sitting at the top. Three equal partners was the construct but even a three-piece band needs a lead singer and Craig was the front man in all senses.

They fell silent. He was right. Tony had apparently dealt with it and given them the all clear. Tony was their Mr Fix-it. He was there just in case they had to sort out something beyond their capabilities. They had kept him on a cash retainer for the last two years and so far they had never had to call on his services. That was until last month. Since then he had earned every penny. This topic had been uppermost in each of their minds for the last few weeks. It was all consuming but Tony had given them the all clear and so they were back in Zurich. Craig was keen to put it behind them all and move forward.

'Anyway guys, that's me,' he broke the silence. 'I'm off to bed. Knackered, 8.30 tomorrow ok?' he said, placing his bulb shaped glass on the heavy oak table and standing up stretching.

James and Ewan nodded. He picked up his overcoat and laptop bag and left the small bar.

With Craig gone Ewan leaned over. 'What do *you* think?'

'Dunno, it's pretty serious. I think. I mean, they *looked* serious to me but I haven't got a fucking clue.'

'I know. You trust Tony?' his voice had a tension which the liquor hadn't subdued.

Shaking his head, 'Dunno, trust Craig though,' James replied.

'Aye,' Ewan said nodding.

There wasn't anything else to say which hadn't already been

said. The problem had been analysed from every conceivable angle. Initially they had all panicked but eventually it had become just another problem to solve. It could have been a business issue and Tony led them through it one evening. Firstly they looked at whether they were a real, a genuine risk or not. They then outlined every possible action they could take, its likelihood of success and the possible reactions. Tony facilitated this in his own unique way but he was very thorough nontheless. Then they moved to how they had found out and came to the conclusion – unless it was one of the four persons present in the room that evening it must have been one of the target companies. They wrapped the evening up by walking again through the various potential responses and settled on a visit by Tony, 'The fire with fire solution,' he wrote this down on the whiteboard theatrically with a smile. He seemed very pleased with this outcome.

This visit had taken place two weeks ago and it was all sorted according to Tony.

James sat there cupping his drink, not sure what else to say. He then quite suddenly drained his glass and stood up, 'Don't stay up too late, busy day tomorrow. Heading out?'

'Dunno. Maybe.'

'Ok, well see you tomorrow.'

Ewan nodded and continued to stare at the roaring fire.

James left the bar and walked through the reception area towards the lift and his bed. He was very tired and the heavy dinner plus the strong booze allowed him the luxury of falling dead asleep almost instantly. He had barely managed to drag his clothes off. Outside the dark river glistened.

Ewan drained his glass and stood up.

He looked around the room. There was only an elderly couple sharing the bar with him now. They sat apart not talking. It was a quiet night in the hotel. Ewan walked from the bar, pulling on his overcoat as he strode past reception. He stepped out of the hotel into the bitterly cold night.

The Limmat river is the main body of water running through the city of Zurich. Its fast-flowing crystal clear waters separate the old town from the main shopping district. Churches, cafés and restaurants line its banks either side as it takes a direct route through the city towards the Zurichsee, one of Switzerland's many lakes. In the summer months the river, and the riverside area is a magnet for tourists and locals alike to swim, have dinner, jog or simply amble along its banks. As city-centre rivers go it is remarkably free of shopping trolleys and the other flotsam and jetsam which would ordinarily find its way into the water.

James sat in the breakfast room staring out over the water as early morning commuters passed by, hunched up against the biting early morning cold. The river looked dark despite the bright morning sun. Even with all the discussions and a good eight hours of sleep the issue was still bugging him. It wouldn't go away. Something told him it was anything but sorted, regardless of Tony and Craig's assurances. The evening they had spent with him wasn't reassuring. It was as if they had missed one big piece of the puzzle but they were all too happy to accept it and move on. The dots were there but somehow he couldn't join them up. He knew the answer must be simple. They usually were.

They expected a call from a procurement manager or chief buyer or even the finance director. This was all part of the longer term plan but to date they had heard nothing. Their encounter with two low-level heavies from Glasgow's underbelly came as a total surprise. Out of the blue. It didn't make any sense. The only weak link James could think of was Tony but Craig was adamant he wasn't the reason. Tony didn't really know enough anyway and these two thugs had known exactly what to say. They had too much information for it to be Tony. Was it really one of the four companies as they had decided? It was logical but still didn't sound right to him. How *did* they find out and why did they enlist the help of the men they met? This didn't seem right according to James. He felt the real answer was rattling around somewhere in his brain. He sat there staring at the river willing it to come to him.

'Alright?' Craig broke his thoughts as he put his jacket and on the back of the seat opposite. 'No Ewan?'

'Not yet, be here shortly I guess,' James replied.

'Better be, I want to get this done quickly and head off,' Craig said as he headed towards the self-service table offering an assortment of bread, cheese and cold meats.

James just nodded and sipped his coffee as he watched his friend enthusiastically help himself. Craig was dressed immaculately as usual wearing a light brown suit and dark tie. His dark hair was cropped short, neat and functional. He wore dark-rimmed glasses. With classical good looks and a slim physique he looked the consummate professional. James was dressed in similar fashion but somehow didn't carry it off as well and he knew this. Craig always looked immaculate and just right, regardless of what he was wearing.

They had business in town today that required the suits. A perfect camouflage in a city full of bankers and finance people. Once done they were driving up to the mountains for a weekend's skiing and fun.

They, or rather the company, owned a ski-apartment up there.

Fifteen minutes later Ewan turned up looking a little tired and ruffled. No one asked why, they simply drained their coffee and left. Ewan grabbed a banana and a muffin, to go.

Their destination was the Alt-Yverdon Bank which has a small physical presence in downtown Zurich. A larger office simply wasn't required with most of their clientele residing outside of Switzerland. The office is situated at the end of Bahnhofstrasse on the banks of the lake. It takes up the whole ground floor of an 18th-century building which had been converted to apartments some fifty years earlier. As Zurich city residences go it's as good as it gets. A quiet and leafy street five minutes' walk from the centre of town. Other than the brass plaque next to the buzzer there is no outward sign of the bank's existence. At first glance it appears to be just another well-to-do apartment. Financially and relatively speaking it's a small bank. Its assets being only a tiny percentage of the larger, more public Swiss banks like Credit Suisse or UBS. Since it was founded by Andre Yverdon in 1847 it had grown steadily, acquiring clients, retaining a certain proximity to them and taking full advantage of the range of specific Swiss banking laws. It is the sort of Swiss bank which has particular clients; it caters to people who value anonymity and a personal service. It is also very specialised.

It continued its steady growth up until the 11th September 2001. Since that day the bank has seen the demand for its services soar exponentially.

Andreas Rogenmoser met them at the door with a strong handshake and a friendly smile. He had been their banker almost since the beginning. James had made the initial contact and Andreas managed their finances ever since. They all walked inside. It was quiet, they could have been forgiven for thinking Andreas was the only employee. The office had the ambiance of a very, very, quiet library. A few jackets and scarves on the hanger next to the door were the only indication there actually were other people in the building. Certainly the services Andreas and Alt-Yverdon offered were not unique but these services were also not easy to find, nor commonplace and the silence in the office reflected the bank's quiet, unassuming approach to doing business. For their services they charged a significant premium over their high street counterparts. Their rates were the equivalent of a backstreet money launderer, but they earned it. And they dressed better on the proceeds James thought as they all followed Andreas inside.

He led them to a modern-looking meeting room. It was small, eight seats and a polished wooden table. A projector hung from the ceiling. Andreas looked exactly as he should, a small man, probably in his mid to late 40s James would have guessed. He was dressed in a dark suit, muted tie and wore small round glasses. He looked like a banker, nothing out of place and everything understated. He spoke with a German accent, not Swiss. James had wondered if he was actually German even though he carried a very common Swiss surname. In any event they were not friends and it was highly unlikely they would ever socialise to give James the chance to ask such a personal question. Discretion is fundamental in his line of work and thus small talk never progressed beyond the weather.

After they had all agreed the weather was perfect for skiing, Andreas opened up the meeting and then proceeded to carefully and methodically walk them through the spreadsheets which he projected against the white wall left blank for the purpose.

Two hours later, Ewan blinked as he stepped outside the office back into the sunlight and stretched his arms out, 'Can we go have fun now?'

'Abso-fucking-lutely,' was the response.

Chapter 2

Galston sat at the open window of his hotel room, smoking and staring out at the Glasgow street. A heavy, leaden sky threatened rain and cars and people rushed by, heading east towards the city. Everywhere he looked he could see cranes and billboards hiding messy construction behind. He sat quietly and looked around. His old stomping ground was slowly being demolished and replaced by new offices and modern flats. Glass and steel buildings whose foundations were being laid on a cesspit of drugs, prostitution, crime and death he thought to himself. He tried to overlay his current view with a memory of how it once was, tried to place the buildings and streets he knew so well but it was impossible. The building site and new buildings totally altered even the direction of streets and thus utterly obliterated the possibility of recognising what was once there. Probably on purpose he thought to himself as the first few spots of rain gathered on his double-glazed hotel window.

He had memories that went back to the days before the Kingston Bridge. The ugly concrete artery which moves thousands of cars in and out of the city daily. He could remember the old dock which once stood there. Today, in its place, yet another batch of modern riverside flats.

His childhood just behind Anderston Cross was not an unhappy one. It was filled with tenement life. The hustle and bustle of lives lived at very close quarters. As a child it was just an adventure for Galston. The smells and the constant noise. Mad Mick lived on the ground floor. The Burnsides above and across from their flat an Indian family. Their name had disappeared from his memory but their food had not. The smell of curry permeated everything and filled the close. They would feed him at least once a week when his own parents forgot to come home at the appropriate time. On these evenings he would stay there playing with their son a year older than him until he heard the sound of his parents staggering home. They would leave the door open and he would wait some time before venturing inside. There was no violence as far as he could remember. They were happy drunks; but drunks all the same. Normally they would be asleep when he crept in and he would crawl between them into the only bed in the flat. The room was filled with musty beer smell and snoring. Even now, when he walked into a pub, the smell would make him relax. A happy reflex memory which made the lines on his face crease into a smile.

He looked west, towards where the tall crumbling tenements had once stood. They had been replaced by a concrete maze of flyovers, walkways and the motorway, the M8, rising up as it approached the bridge. The motorway was the death of Galston's childhood. A scorched-earth policy of motorway building left nothing in its wake and as it moved slowly west it took with it districts and neighbourhoods in their entirety.

One day, Galston's street simply disappeared and they were relocated to a high rise in Drumchapel. This was where the darkness first appeared.

He looked across at the tall building going up directly opposite his hotel. The Argyle Building. The billboard showed a picture of a modern high rise. Executive apartments for executive people with executive lifestyles, whatever the fuck that means he thought flicking the cigarette out of the window and lighting another.

He could easily pinpoint the moments in his life when he made choices, choices which put him on a certain path. He could see the map clearly. How he got to where he was today, a winding path with each intersection a choice, a conscious deliberate choice. Life was simply a matter of choices to Galston. Choose to smoke, choose to go to university, choose to go home or stay out, choose to study hard or fuck about. The critical part is recognising this and then being able to live with the consequences. It's your fault if you are unhappy, poor, an alcoholic or a bus driver. Don't fucking blame me.

One evening Galston stood over the prone body of a young man. It was 1972; the man had done nothing wrong really. He made the mistake of staying in the pub long after most sensible men would have left. Galston stood over him as he lay on a bed of paper sacks filled with concrete in a half-built car park stairwell. Dust covered everything, his hair, his clothes, his eyebrows. Blood flowed from various parts of the young man's face. It was puffed up, swollen and unrecognisable. His left arm stuck out at an abnormal angle to the rest of his body. Galston stood over him breathing hard and made a choice.

He had no regrets, he chose this life. He knew with certainty that he could have had another life. He was smart enough, but he chose this one, and that was that.

There was a twinge of nostalgia as he watched the spindly cranes moving, towering over what was left of the Anderston Centre. At sixty years old he just assumed the nostalgia came with the territory of being an old man.

The phone beside his bed rang, jolting him from his memories. His taxi for the airport had arrived.

He flicked away his cigarette, drained the coffee from his mug, and left the room dragging a huge trolley bag behind him.

Three hours later dwarfed in the glass and steel cathedral of London Heathrow Terminal 5 he sat drinking coffee waiting for his connecting flight. He watched as the crowds killed time. He watched them mill around, browsing the shops and the multitude of options to spend money before flying. They were trapped in an ergonomically designed kill zone of shops, restaurants and bars. He could almost see the shopkeepers wringing their hands with glee. He hated it and just sat there feeling horribly out of place. He was never supposed to exist in this antiseptic wipe clean world. He tried to imagine what they thought when they looked at him and came up with nothing. Just another old man probably. This is the world for the people moving into Anderston, the next generation. He assumed they would be better than the last. They had to be.

They were all shapes, sizes and colours. In the time he had been sitting there he reckoned he had seen every race on earth. A blaze of colour and noise passed him by as he sat there quietly trying to blend in.

The television above him showed his flight to Zurich was boarding. He left the coffee bar and walked slowly to his gate. Down on the main concourse he sensed an atmosphere. He couldn't pinpoint it precisely but it was there, definitely. As he walked a child ran across his path and he had to stop suddenly to avoid accidently kicking the little boy. The child's mother ran over looking at him and smiling apologetically. She raised her eyebrows and mouthed 'I'm sorry' before grabbing the child and pulling him back to the relative safety of the seated area. Galston nodded and continued walking towards his gate. As he approached he could see the queue forming for the ground staff to check tickets and passports. The queue was largely made up of men, wearing suits.

Galston stopped and looked back towards the main concourse and the throng of people. He suddenly realised why he didn't fit in, what was keeping him from joining the crowds, what that feeling was as he left the coffee bar. He realised it and he accepted it.

He turned around, fished his boarding card and passport from his jacket pocket and joined the back of the queue.

Four hundred miles north, across the street from Galston's hotel, a wrecking ball broke through a ground floor retaining wall and the thirty eight-year-old multi-story car park which was standing in the way of a new office block, collapsed. Thirty tonnes of concrete and steel settled into a haphazard pile awaiting removal. The rain quickly settled the cloud of dust. A graffiti covered concrete block from an old stairwell had broken in half under the sheer weight falling on top of it revealing a human femur. It stuck out vertically, white and glistening in the dull grey light. Scraps of denim and fabric were pressed into the concrete which had encased it for so long. From a distance it was just another shard of metal in a sea of building debris.

It stood there clearly for five minutes before the wrecking ball returned and turned it to dust.

Chapter 3

James sat on the packed snow speaking on his phone. In front of him was a brilliant white Alpine vista and he squinted behind his sunglasses as he looked around.

Slate-grey rocky cliffs lined the high Alpine bowl. All around the perimeter cable cars and tow lifts deposited their passengers at the various drop off points. Individually and collectively they turned, regrouped, sorted their poles and their bags before choosing their route of descent, letting gravity do the rest. They meandered their way down the mountain, turning and stopping, speeding straight, crouching with their arms tucked in or carving and looping across the perfectly groomed slopes. It had snowed lightly the night before and the hard-packed base had a two-inch, icing-sugar layer on top. Young children flew down, oblivious to the danger. They laughed at the older skiers who gracefully picked their route. Families skied in formation and a troupe from the local ski school snaked like an Alpine conga, fifteen persons deep.

James watched them. Lyndsey was home sick and she had wanted to speak to him. He could hear Sarah and her fiancé talking in the background. It was an agitated conversation. He knew Craig was somewhere further down the mountain and could still see Ewan's large frame ambling sideways on his snowboard towards the next crest. He sat there, leaning against a snow pile, basking in the sun as he talked to his daughter. She had demanded that she be allowed to speak with him. James had apologised to Sarah before speaking with her but was pleased she had done so. The heated discussion going on in the background pleased him even more, nothing more than schaden-freude but it made him smile nonetheless.

He talked to his daughter and sunbathed.

Without realising it since their arrival a few hours earlier in the mountain resort James had not thought about the "issue". This would have surprised him given his preoccupation over the last few weeks. The world at that moment, in the life of James Bisset, was a very good one indeed. He smiled to himself as his daughter explained why she must be able to stay up till 10pm on a school night. He neither agreed, nor disagreed. Taking a neutral position. He listened and said the odd 'uhuh', or 'I know princess' whenever she stopped to take a breath. She was only venting, she knew her biological father didn't make the rules and in no way could he change them. His role was mostly a listening one now during their calls and conversations. He just assumed it was her age. He also assumed this was the norm for father/daughter relationships at this point in their lives irrespective of living arrangements.

In any event he was happy with how things were shaping up with his children. Rose was six years old and had never really known a life with him in it permanently. Sarah had taken them out of his life when she was barely two years old. She would run giggling excitedly towards him when he turned up on their doorstep. To her, Daddy picking them up on a Friday and dropping them off on drop-off Sunday was all she knew and seemed content with that. Lyndsey was different. She had reacted badly to the whole affair and James had to admit Sarah handled this admirably, even if she was the reason they were separating in the first place. Take that smelly elephant out of the room and James had a lot of respect for how she handled the children. It was how it was, and James now couldn't imagine life with Sarah and the kids in it permanently. He would never admit that to anyone but life goes on and James's had moved on. He kept nodding and interjecting with the odd word or two but his mind was elsewhere. She didn't need to know that.

Lyndsey hung up after telling him she loved him too and he sat there admiring the view for a further few minutes. The air was freezing cold despite the sun. He could see his breath and the cold from the snow was creeping through the four layers of clothing he was wearing.

After a short time he picked himself up, clicked into his skis and headed down the piste to catch up with his friends. He took the direct route and found them waiting for him at a makeshift ski bar.

'All ok?' Ewan asked him, passing over a Styrofoam mug filled with a red steaming liquid.

'Aye fine, just Lynds whinging bout her mum.' He sipped the warm liquid and looked around. There were only a handful of people congregating around the bar. It was mid-week. The hard-core party crew would arrive tomorrow evening.

'Snow's fantastic,' Craig said looking back up the mountain. 'Hope the weather lasts out.'

The other two nodded and sipped their drinks, in the freezing temperatures the boiling liquid quickly cooled.

'What about tonight?' James asked.

'I'm going out, don't know about you two,' Craig responded.

'I am,' Ewan said.

'Guess we're going out then,' James said smiling, and finished his drink. He started moving back towards the piste.

'I'm off, meet you back there later.'

'The fuck you going?' Craig shouted after him.

James didn't answer. He pointed with a ski pole towards another peak across the bowl. It was mostly un-pisted so he was going alone.

Craig and Ewan watched him depart.

James was the most accomplished skier of them all having been dragged up to the freezing, windswept Cairngorms in his youth and the only one who could with any level of confidence manage some of the more challenging runs in the area. He enjoyed the freedom and exploration that going off piste offered him. The feeling of rushing through deep powder. Snow up around his knees, feeling the contours of the ground below but not seeing them. He loved the challenge and the sense of danger. If it really existed. He had never actually been caught in a tricky situation but was acutely aware of the risk. He skied down and then started a long traverse of tow bars and ski lifts which would eventually deposit him at the top of a two-kilometre patch of untouched powder.

He stood at the top breathing in the freezing air deeply and scanning the horizon. Soaking up the view and plotting his route down before setting off for his final run of the day.

* * *

The Broken Bar wasn't really as broken as its name suggested but was the sort of establishment which had been purposely designed to withstand a lot of punishment. At some point in its history it probably did deserve its name located as it was in the vaulted cellar of a hotel. It was dark with a cave feel about it. Rough plaster covered the ceilings and walls. Wooden barrels served as tables and there was the odd seat but mostly everyone stood. In any event for most nights in season it was standing room only and even on a Thursday when it was 2/3 full there was limited room to move around. After midnight they regularly had to turn people away. Loud rock music was the staple diet of its patrons and tonight was no exception. There was a four-piece band crowded into a small corner blasting out cover songs, cycling through the classics of rock. Loudly.

Craig stood in the corner drinking beer from a bottle and surveying the room. James was jumping up and down in front of the band and Ewan had left sometime earlier for the casino. Craig's legs were aching, his face was flushed red. He felt drunk. He was drunk and he giggled to himself as he watched his friend jump around like a madman. James's only saving grace was that everyone else was doing exactly the same thing.

In a mad world, only the mad are sane, he thought. This again made him giggle to himself. 'The philosopher drunk,' he said out loud and he giggled some more.

'Es ist laut,' a voice shouted from just beside him.

He spun round to see her standing there smiling at him.

'Sorry?' he replied, his voice lost in the din of ACDC.

'Es ist laut!' she shouted again still smiling.

Craig held his hands up apologetically.

'Entschuldigung, ich nicht sprechen Deutsch, sorry,' he replied using his standard abysmal German. She was stunning, he thought.

'English?' She smiled back at him.

He smiled and held his beer bottle up, she did the same and they touched glasses, 'Prost.'

Craig looked at her. She was beautiful, dark black hair, loosely curled, dark thick-rimmed designer glasses. About the same height as him wearing a blue dress and knee-high boots. She leaned against the cave wall and drank from the neck of her beer bottle.

'Yes, English, sorry,' he said grinning like a madman.

'It's ok, I know the English can only speak one language, something to do with the school system over there I hear,' she shouted over the noise, smiling. Her English was perfect if heavily accented.

'Wouldn't know, am Scottish,' he shouted back, the grin still fixed to his face.

She indicated towards James who at that moment was playing air guitar on his knees in front of the lead singer 'Your friend? I saw you earlier,' she spoke directly into his ear to avoid the need to shout.

Craig looked over at James and then turned back 'No fucking way. Him? No, nothing to do with me.' He had to lean towards her to speak and shook his head solemnly as he did.

She looked confused, 'Really?'

'Yes, just likes to follow me around. Canna get rid of him.'

'Oh, ok,' she frowned.

'Course not, kidding. Yes, he's with me.' He added, 'Just not right now. Especially when he does that,' pointing behind him towards the band. This was hardly a Judas moment and in any event James would have happily disowned Craig in the blink of an eye had the circumstances been reversed. She is truly beautiful he thought again for the third time in as many minutes.

She smiled at him and held out her hand, 'Sabine.'

He took it. 'Craig, pleased to meet you.'

'Like in James Bond?' she asked.

'Daniel Craig? Aye that's me, James Bond. Here by yourself, Sabine?'

Before she could answer they were interrupted by a loud cheer as the band finished the song and announced a short break.

Craig could feel his body sway slightly. He was trying hard to appear less drunk than he actually was. He leaned back against the cave wall to steady himself but his mind, dulled with alcohol, had forgotten he had turned around to speak and moved away from the wall.

The mob at the bar doubled as soon as the band stopped. James looked around disorientated. He could taste the salty sweat covering his face and his thin shirt was soaked through and stuck to his chest. His jeans felt sticky and he needed a beer. He looked around for Craig and saw him and the girl. He did not recognise her. He could see Craig move backwards. It looked initially as if his friend was going to turn. Instead he kept leaning backwards and then, for no discernible reason as far as James could see, he fell backwards. Hard onto the floor. One moment he was standing there. The next he was falling down leaning forward as he did so as if he was trying to sit on thin air. He spilled his beer.

James pushed his way through the crowd of people and made it to Craig just as he was pulling himself up. The girl looked concerned but stood back as he arrived.

'Fuck you doing?' James asked, helping him up.

'Trying to not look like an idiot,' was Craig's response as he straightened his clothes and wiped beer from his shirt.

'How's that going then?' Craig replied deadpan watching him rub his jeans.

Craig looked at him and then at Sabine and started giggling again. He hugged James. It was a drunk man hug.

'Who are you?' James asked pushing Craig away and turning to Sabine, his tone was friendly.

'Sabine,' she said offering her hand smiling. She was a little subdued given the last few seconds but had not left. A fact not lost on Craig.

'James,' James said, shaking her hand.

'Also as in Bond,' Craig interjected.

'Not confusing then,' she said, adding, 'Nice dancing James,' nodding towards the dance floor area.

'Thanks. Never had a lesson,' he replied gleefully. 'Am off for a beer, catch you two later.'

Before they could say anything he left them, heading back into the crowd. He surveyed the mosh pit in front of the wooden bar, it was eight people deep. Deciding he didn't need a beer that desperately he pushed his way towards the cloakroom. As he waited for his jacket to be retrieved, he sent an SMS to Craig.

Good luck, cu tomorrow, J.

* * *

One hundred kilometres west of the Broken Bar, Galston pushed open the door to his hotel room and dragged his heavy luggage inside. He looked around, took his jacket off, and sat down on the bed.

His phone beeped and vibrated an SMS.

Still ok for tomorrow?

Galston responded positively then lay flat on the starched

counterpane. It was late and he was tired. He had ended up in a middle seat on his flight from London. Sandwiched between two Swiss bankers trying unsuccessfully to hold a conversation over him. He could have offered to move but didn't. He just sat there drinking beer, ignoring them and staring around the cabin as the plane bumped and lurched its way through the winter storms hanging over central Europe. By the time he reached his destination for the day he was very tired.

He rolled off the bed, undressed and pulled the duty free bottle of malt he had picked up in Glasgow from his bag. Pouring himself a generous measure he climbed into bed and turned the light off.

* * *

Sometime later James woke up with a jolt. He was dreaming deeply but something had awoken him. A sound. A noise. Something had broken through the fog of sleep and triggered an alarm in his head. He quietly rolled out of the single bed he was sleeping in. The bed across the room was empty. It was Craig's bed. He checked his watch. 4.47am. A noise in the living room took his attention and he crept slowly out of the bedroom, holding his breath and pulling the door back very slowly. Ewan was sitting on the couch.

'Fuck's sake Ewan, scared the shite outta me,' he said walking into the room, 'what you doing?'

'Drinking. That ok with you?' he said, holding up a whisky glass.

'Jesus Christ,' he laughed and flopped down on the couch. 'Any luck?'

Ewan shook his head. 'Naw, never is.'

'How much?' James asked.

'Nae much. Fun though,' Ewan sipped his dram. 'Craig back?' he said, quickly changing the subject.

James shook his head. 'Naw, left him with some German bird at the Broken.'

Ewan laughed and sat back on the couch.

'It's always Craig. Shit. If Susan ever cottons on.'

'Uhuh, anyhow I'm off to bed again. Try to keep quiet eh?'

'Fanny.' Ewan toasted him with his whisky glass and then downed the dram in one gulp.

Ewan didn't choose to be an addict. He didn't sit down one day and decide he would throw away every penny he earned. He didn't decide this consciously but he did it as surely as if he had actually sat down and planned it with meticulously detail. He was an addict and hated himself because he knew he was. His personality type drove him down the more of everything route and he did just that. He would regularly keep going until he fell down, lost all his money or the girl left the room once her meter ran out. Invariably it was a combination of all three which would eventually persuade him to stop. Until the next time that was. It was all relative but his single most expensive vice was gambling. The other vices would surely kill him, but gambling would guarantee he did so a pauper.

When Orchid landed at his feet Ewan's life and his addictions accelerated. He could now afford the lifestyle he had dreamed of and his personality craved. And he indulged it with a gusto that frightened even himself. But he couldn't stop. How much is enough? This was a question he couldn't answer. So he just kept going. Pushing the boundaries and consuming everything that came his way.

He knew it. But didn't stop it. He tried to analyse himself and came to the conclusion that he was bored. Normal life; work, girlfriend, shopping, kids, telly, holidays in Majorca, nice car, garden and soft furniture bored him. He opted out of the constituent parts of a typical normal life and chose an alternative. He imagined himself like a factory fishing boat emptying the oceans; he scooped up everything in his way before moving on, leaving it bare and empty. He chose it, Orchid paid for it and he hated himself for it.

This hatred reached a low point two years ago. The night he paralysed Maria.

It was accidental of course, most of the events in Ewan's life were. It was an accident, but this was little comfort to Maria Matowski as she lay on the bed willing her legs to move. He initially thought it was another one of the games they would play and stood at the foot of the bed watching her with an interested grin. But as her voice became more desperate and her upper body flexed and twisted he realised it was the end of playtime. He untied her and tried in vain to figure out what was wrong. He found out a few hours later in the Edinburgh Royal Infirmary. A tired-looking young female doctor came out and explained that Maria was suffering from a form of sudden paraplegia, brought on from severe spinal cord compression. They would operate immediately but couldn't guarantee any success. Odds? She shook her head and shrugged her shoulders. As she turned away from him heading back to the operating room he walked in the opposite direction. He walked out of the hospital leaving Maria to her operation, her rehabilitation and her ultimate deportation back to Slovakia.

His self-hatred became a loathing but he didn't stop. Maria became Svetlana, Daisy or Mary-Bell. It didn't really matter to him. He continued to consume everything at an increasingly ferocious rate. He consumed and hid it. He kept on consuming, hiding and hating himself right up until the day Marias "owner" knocked at the door of his cheap one-bedroomed rented flat. This is when the guilt started.

The sunlight, which burst through into the room as James unwound the metal shutters the following morning, was biblical in its brightness. He looked around the room. Craig was asleep on the other bed, fully clothed, deeply asleep. James opened the window wide and walked through to the living room. It was

10.30am.

He had a serious hangover thirst and drank deeply from the kitchen tap before turning on the coffee machine. He could hear Craig loudly complaining with some choice words about the Arctic air filling the bedroom. Smiling he headed towards the bathroom, knocking loudly on Ewan's door as he passed.

Thirty minutes later the three of them were sitting drinking coffee debriefing. James listened as the two of them swapped stories and laughed. James knew he was the only one going to venture out onto the snow that day. Craig looked a mess and in any event was still dressed as he was the evening before. Ewan showed no intention either. He ate a croissant and sipped his coffee as his friends talked and then left them to their story-telling.

James carried his skis and walked a ski-boot robot walk towards the cable car at the bottom of the road.

* * *

Galston was already on the move. He woke early, dressed in the ski clothes he had picked up the week before in Glasgow, and left the hotel. He had a print out of the train times. It was an easy journey and as James was boarding the cable car, Galston sipped coffee and watched the Alpine scenery fly by. His eyes squinted against the bright sunlight and his mind drifted.

It drifted to Drumchapel one evening in the summer of 1969. Galston was seventeen years old. He often thought about this night. He had just started work at the Goodyear Tyre factory. A heavy labouring job but it paid, and for the first time in his life, he felt the freedom of independence. He had money in his pocket and was old enough to spend it on things. Adult things. He knew the date, July 22nd. He knew this because the day before he and his friend Thomas (Tam) Hellman had watched, along with half of the world's population, Neil Armstrong step from the lunar module Eagle onto the surface of the moon. It was a balmy summer's evening and they kicked a ball back and forth between themselves. Either side of them two tower blocks rose up. When Galston thought of this evening there was always a soundtrack, Jimi Hendrix, The Who, Creedence Clearwater Revival. The music varied but it was always there. He knew it was his mind playing tricks on him, but as he watched himself and Tam kick the ball, in his memory the music would always be there.

He had known Tam ever since they moved to Drumchapel. They went to school together and now that they were grown up, they went to work together. Tam had started with Goodyear two weeks after Galston. They were very close but very different. Tam's family roots were in Sweden. He had a shock of blond hair and would have been the model of Aryan perfection if it wasn't for the poor diet which had stunted his growth and left him looking pale, skinny and malnourished. Galston was darker, taller and heavier. Standing next to Tam, Galston was a robust picture of health and vitality. They came of age together but both knew their paths from this point on would start to diverge.

Tam could run like the wind and play football. Really play. Galston couldn't remember a day which didn't involve Tam and a football. It was almost a permanent extension to his rake thin body. He was going for a trial with St Mirren the following Sunday and Galston had no doubt whatsoever that he would succeed.

Galston's future was with Goodyear or similar. He was built for the work and deep down he liked the physical aspects of it. He earned his money with sweat and this seemed right to him.

There was no jealousy between them, though. He was genuinely happy for Tam but he also knew this would be the start of the end of their friendship. Tam had talked excitedly about the trial that evening he remembered and Galston talked about the moon landings.

The music would build up to a crescendo in his head and his

memory always jumped to a few hours later. It would jump to Tam lying on the concrete next to the swing, his head squashed into an abnormally flat shape. Blond hair and thick blood. Galston lay next to him, his foot dangling limply on a swing. He lay there quietly, not moving, not feeling his own pain. He lay there and watched blood ooze from Tam's ears and the life disappear from his skinny friend's eyes. This was when the darkness appeared.

'Fahrkarten bitte.'

He was jolted back to the present by the ticket inspector and the images rushed from his mind.

* * *

Thirty kilometres east of Galston, Craig crawled back into bed and Ewan made himself another cup of coffee. James exited the aging cable car and stood again at the top of his run. The air was freezing this side of the mountain. It was westerly facing and thus almost permanently kept in the shade. He pulled his scarf up over his nose and his woolly hat down level with his eyebrows. He fitted his goggles, adjusted his rucksack, and slipped his gloved hands through the loops on his ski poles. Below him he could see the marks he had made the day before and visually he tried to plot a different route down. He saw a route where the snow remained untouched and with a confident push on his poles disappeared over the edge.

Chapter 4

Craig had approached James. It was his idea.

Five years ago, a warm Friday evening in July. In a pub just off Rose Street they met, as they always did after work. It was a routine they had fallen into after leaving university and barring illness, holiday or a girl distracting them, it was an appointment they never missed.

That evening the pub was filled with an eclectic mix of business men and women winding down after a long week and tourists soaking up the overall Scottish-ness of the place. It was summertime, noisy, smoky and smelled just as a pub should. People jostled to catch the eye of the three over worked barmaids sweating behind the long mahogany bar and every table was filled. The ancient wooden floor was sticky and slippery in equal measure. James and Craig occupied a booth. They both sipped pints.

'I've an idea,' Craig said, and this was how it started. 'I've an idea,' he repeated. 'A fucking good one.'

'Go on then will you, what's your *fucking* good idea this time?' James responded sarcastically. Craig always had ideas. Most of them were related to giving up work, starting a business and retiring before they turned fifty. Most of the ideas were also about as likely to happen as the pair of them travelling to Mars. James had good reason to be sceptical.

It was a game they played, Craig had an idea, James mocked it. These were the rules.

Craig then proceeded to explain the fundamentals of his idea. It was designed to be 90% benevolent with the remaining 10% to do with as they wished. It was a Robin Hood for the modern era as he called it and as usual James mocked it mercilessly.

That was until Craig spoke again.

'Set it up a month ago.'

'Aye right, course you have.'

Craig then took a sheet of paper out of the bag at his feet. It was a crumpled bank statement. He smoothed it out in front of James, slowly and carefully, ignoring the beer which started soaking into it.

'Fuck off,' James said, but he studied the damp bank statement anyway. There wasn't much to study. Only four entries. The first entry titled Initial Deposit was for £10 and dated a month ago. The remaining three entries only had numerical descriptions but the closing balance, as of yesterday, was £10,747.

'Like I said,' Craig said sitting back in his seat and clasping his hands behind his head.

'Winding me up, right?'

'Nope,' Craig said, reaching for his glass. 'Need your help though.'

'Ok?' James replied. He was serious now and took a long slug from his glass before Craig launched into a ten-minute monologue.

James listened without any questions. He followed Craig, process step by process step. Craig talked and supplemented the descriptions with beer mat diagrams. They were both familiar with the processes having worked on a number of similar projects. It was simple. Its simplicity was what made it beautiful. Overcomplicate something and it stands out, be bold and just do it, it will fly through, Craig told him. No one will even know. Craig stopped speaking and smiled, 'Well?'

James sat back. He looked around the bar. People were talking, laughing, relaxing. The mix of loud conversations created an incomprehensible din. It was clearly English but no discernible words could be made out. James watched the happy Friday crowd and thought about what Craig had just told him. This was pure and simple theft, but this didn't bother him. What bothered him was it was real. It stepped over the fantasy line they had always danced around. Talking about something was very different to *actually* doing it and what was worse Craig had already crossed the line and was looking back holding his hand out urging him to jump. James sat there quietly looking at his friend as he slowly and persuasively talked him into following him. He knew he would, the alarm bells were ringing but how could he do anything else?

The following morning he woke with a hangover.

He was staying in a small rented flat in Stockbridge in the north of the city at the time. He walked through to the bathroom, as he stood at the toilet swaying slightly the evening's conversation came back to him in a rush. The cold light of day gave everything a dull grey complexion and within ten minutes he found himself swearing loudly at Craig on the telephone. He was swearing but never once reversed his decision to follow him friend off the cliff.

It was at that time, five years ago, on that warm and drunken summer evening in Edinburgh, that their company, Orchid, was born. It was so named after a lengthy discussion. Ultimately they decided on the name because it was clean, simple and unthreatening. This was an image they wanted to convey.

Their first company was already "on stream" as Craig called it. He used a lot of oil industry metaphors. It just seemed appropriate. They were prospecting for money and when they found a source, they started pumping it before moving on. James followed suit and adopted the terminology.

Holmes PLC, was a leading global manufacturer in the consumer electronics industry. Headquartered in Boston they were a global concern and had their European Headquarters in Geneva, Switzerland. Craig had chosen it for two reasons. Firstly he knew their ERP (Enterprise Resource System) well. An ERP system sits at the heart of the business. The systematic glue that binds everything together. Everything about Holmes was managed through their ERP system. A customer order is received and it is entered into the system. This sends a signal to the warehouse to pick the goods. Once the warehouse picks the goods the system generates a shipping notification and once shipped an invoice is sent to the customer via email. Two humans are involved in the whole process, from order receipt to invoicing. One to enter the order and one to pick it from the warehouse shelf. The system manages the rest. Finance, accounting, warehousing, planning, human resources everything is booked and managed through the system. Everything was inextricably linked and Craig knew this system intimately – he designed it.

The second reason for choosing Holmes was that he didn't like them. And that, according to Craig was as good a reason as any.

Once he had adjusted the data which supported the ERP system and created a new supplier, Orchid, he then went about creating the necessary electronic paperwork. He created an order, booked the receipt of the fictitious goods into their warehouse. On the financial side once the order had been approved, which in this case it was – he approved it himself – and the goods had been received, payment was an automatic process. The invoice was matched to the receipt and the order and the money flowed out of the Holmes bank account straight to Orchid's.

The next step was to remove the evidence. In this case the evidence would be the lack of goods sitting on a warehouse shelf. What they didn't need was an overzealous warehouseman deciding to take a look at the products which the system said were on the shelf. Craig wrote it off, essentially the electronic equivalent of putting it in the bin. The key was keep it small and infrequent. Keep the write offs small enough to not be double checked and this was where James stepped in. This was their tripwire moment, the moment when they were exposed. It needed to be planned and timed to not raise any alarm bells. Given the size and complexity of Holmes PLC James was reasonably certain the sums they were pumping were not significant enough to create a noticeable spike but he was extremely cautious anyway. It was in his nature.

Once they started, it became easier. The company suddenly had a history with Orchid and thus it had less chance of appearing out of the ordinary, the longer it went on the more it became part of their bona-fide business. Another major hurdle was financial year-end. Once a year the company's books were checked and reviewed by an independent audit firm. James made sure that Orchid's transactions were well below the materiality level for the audit. The level at which these auditors starting to take an interest. Once they were 4 months clear of the first year-end, Craig and James set about automating the process. They then moved onto company number two. Holmes PLC was left to its own devices, pumping out money at purposely set irregular intervals. James would check the receipts once a month or so and that was that. Nice, simple and very profitable.

Company number two proved a more interesting proposition for James. From his perspective it was the first he would be involved in from the start and secondly, he knew exactly which company it would be.

Setting up an Orchid transaction totally from the outside wasn't impossible but definitely beyond the skills James and Craig had. They relied on having an inside view of the system. They relied on knowing its flaws and the degree to which the organisation had managed to drive through efficient processes. For efficient processes means limited human input and a system with limited human input is one which gave Orchid its opportunity.

Craig had just finished working for Brown & Bingham Medical , so recently in fact that he still had a login and password for their internal network, and crucially their Oracle based ERP system. He had a window of up to three months before the password would be removed so he had to act immediately.

Brown & Bingham was a Healthcare company with a track record of corruption and dubious contract awards. They made generic drugs, the ones which filled the marketplace once the company who had developed the drug in the first place lost its patent rights.

They traded on price and connections. They were the darlings of governments looking to slash healthcare budgets and loathed by doctors and patients alike. James equally disliked Brown & Bingham and had enough of an inside view to understand its reputation wasn't totally without foundation.

This also made it the ideal company to start a trading relationship with Orchid and within a month it had made its first deposit.

By the time this deposit hit the account the balance stood at £217,567.45 and this became another problem. What to do with the cash? The problem was more how to move the money, where to move the money to and how to account for it. Having such a sum of money isn't necessarily a good thing and James took the time to temper Craig's enthusiasm for the six-figure sum sitting in the account. Craig paced the room like a petulant sulking teenager as he did, but he listened to James's accounting speech all the same. They needed to account for it in such a way that if asked, they could answer the question 'where did it come from?' and be able to provide a suitably believable paper trail to support it. The taxman is a stickler for proof James pointed out to him.

This was when James contacted the Alt Verdon bank and from that moment they had a working process. It wasn't as legal or as financially robust as James would have liked but as Craig reminded him, the whole process wasn't entirely kosher either so this was probably as good as it was going to get.

10% of the revenues flowed through Orchid's official accounts and James created the invoices to support it, consulting invoices for a long list of detailed services. Services which had never been performed.

James incorporated the company and Orchid Ltd became a bona-fide, legitimate company. It paid its taxes like the good corporate citizen it was. The remaining profits in the accounts were paid out to its two shareholders – James and Craig.

The other 90% of the revenues flowed indirectly through another bank account account to Alt Yverdon. Bypassing the taxman's glare.

James wasn't happy but it worked. Considering the construct of Orchid and its sole reason for being even he admitted it was the best they could hope for.

He also admitted to Craig, as he explained the money flows to him one evening, it wasn't as if they had a Plan B.

Chapter 5

Galston stepped off the train onto the platform. He looked around. He was surrounded by people carrying skis, bags and other mountain paraphernalia. Again he felt out of place and began to realise there were very few places he actually felt at ease. The air was dry and cold, his breath filled the air in front of his face and his boots crunched the heavy brown salt layered onto the platform. It was surprisingly clean he thought as he moved with the crowds towards the exit and the taxi sign. He had time but preferred to be early.

James bumped over the lip and landed on the pisted track. He relaxed and let gravity take him, in lazy loops, the remaining 200 meters to the base where a queue was forming for the chair lift. He skied past people walking up towards the queue and stopped on the last available sliver of snow before the car park. Removing his skis he stood there watching the crowds from the train walk towards the taxi queue. Busy weekend he thought to himself and was glad he had managed to get onto the snow before the crowds arrived.

Galston shuffled forward in the queue with his bag. He looked around the huge bowl and could see small dark specks moving through the brilliant white landscape. Just to his left, above the car park, he could see a chairlift and people queuing, waiting to be whisked up the mountain.

Galston stared directly at James. James stared directly back at Galston and for the briefest of moments they locked eyes. Of the two of them it was only Galston who had seen a picture of James and he would have recognised him had he not been wearing a hat and scarf pulled up to his eyes. To Galston, James looked exactly like every other person enjoying the snow. Galston eyes moved on scanning the view, he was genuinely awe struck with the high Alpine scenery. He had never seen anything quite as dramatic or as steep as this before. The cold, the clean thin air, literally took his breath away as he moved slowly forward towards the line of yellow branded taxis.

Galston had only seen photographs of Craig, James and Ewan. He had sent Barry and Dots to meet with them in the first place. They were young and energetic. His assumption was their enthusiasm would be more effective than his traditional approach. He was wrong and this was the reason Sandy had stepped in and told Galston what to do. He thought about how his visit to the town would play out. He had a plan but it was more complicated than normal. It was a pantomime with too many moving parts. It was Sandy's plan and he had a tendency to be a little theatrical. Too many movies Galston thought. His biggest worry was in having to involve someone else. This was something Galston never did. Sandy normally just told him who and sometimes how and then left it up to Galston to figure out the various details. He delegated it to him, he was the boss and that was his job. This time it was different though and Sandy had told him who, how, when, with what and with who. Galston was in this instance just following a recipe. A murderous recipe written by someone else and he didn't like it one bit.

James picked up his skis, placed them on his shoulder and started walking towards the apartment. He passed the taxi queue just as Galston climbed inside the lead car.

'St Anton Hotel,' he said and relaxed back against the leather seat of the Mercedes Benz.

James continued up the hill as the taxi passed him.

* * *

Craig's phone vibrated and he reached over to read the SMS. He was still in bed and scrolled through the messages received. Two messages from his wife and one from Sabine.

I had a gr8 time last night, meet tnight?

Craig smiled remembering the night before. He responded
Hi sxy girl J absolutely!
He closed his eyes and willed himself to go back to sleep.

* * *

The Hotel St Anton is a purpose-built hotel. Constructed to look like an enormous chalet it has two hundred rooms, a few modern function rooms and a wellness centre located on the ground floor. It is built on a hill and thus both the wellness centre and the reception have doors to the outside even though they are separated by two floors inside the hotel. From the pool swimmers can gaze over the snowy mountainous landscape behind the triple glazed windows. Galston's room, on the third floor was in fact only one flight of stairs up from the reception. This was slightly confusing and on his first attempt Galston found himself walking around the fifth floor looking for his room. He eventually found his room and pulled his bag inside. Wooden beams, wooden chairs, a medium-sized bed and a balcony. He walked outside and lit a cigarette. He still had thirty minutes.

* * *

Ewan was lying on the sofa reading a book killing time before the evening started. Ewan loved to read. If it could be added to his long list of addictions it certainly wasn't one he felt bad about. He had fallen in love with books early as a child growing up in Fife. It was a love affair which never left him. The earliest books he could remember were the Famous Five books his mother had bought him for his seventh birthday. He could even remember their covers. He didn't know it but the only time he was totally in a relaxed state without the aid of alcohol or a girl was when he had his nose stuck in a book. Ewan could devour a book every couple of days if he allowed himself to. His preference now were thrillers or historical-based fiction but he wasn't that picky. A book was a book to Ewan. His current book was a thriller of sorts, written by an ex SAS soldier. The author's photo was blacked out on the back cover to add gravitas and an air of authority. It was an easy read. The hero was currently staking out a Russian drug dealer. In true SAS fashion he was dug into a muddy pit close to the house silently watching and gathering data. Ewan idly wondered why he didn't just fix a camera and then retire back to his warm and clean hotel room with pay-per-view movies and a minibar but concluded that probably wouldn't make good reading.

He was dragged from the foxhole by James returning.

'Craig still in bed?' James asked as he noisily removed his jacket and ski trousers.

'Aye, went back just after you left. Busy out there?'

'No, getting that way though, lots of folks arriving. Gonna be busy the weekend.' He padded in his ski socks and thermal long johns to the kitchen and turned the coffee machine back on. He tore a chunk of bread from the French stick lying next to it. It was a little hard having sat there since they arrived yesterday but he was hungry and couldn't be bothered making anything else.

'Snow's good though, icy in the shade but the piste is great,' he said from the kitchen munching on the stale bread.

Ewan nodded at this and said nothing. The snow didn't enthuse him quite as much as it did James. With the exception of his night-time activities, of the three of them he was the least active. His overall appearance reflected this but he brushed it off in the Scottish male way common to men of his size, looks and proclivities. He returned to his book as James busied himself in his periphery.

* * *

Sabine Weinstrom entered the lift of the hotel St Anton and pressed the button for reception. She looked at herself in the mirrored door and was quite happy with what she saw looking back. One or two minor lines around her eyes but apart from that nothing else to show that she had just passed the thirty mark. She wore tight jeans, slip-on shoes and a black roll-neck jumper. She was satisfied with her appearance. Dark hair, with a natural loose curl fell over her shoulders and contrasted well with her milky pale skin.

She pushed her hair back and checked her teeth for lipstick as the lift arrived at reception.

Galston was there waiting for her. She spotted him before he spotted her. He wasn't difficult to spot. He was the only person sitting drinking coffee in the expansive reception area. Everyone else had a reason to be there, sorting luggage, checking in, rounding up kids, carrying skis. Galston sat staring into space. She studied him before approaching. A large man. About sixty or seventy she guessed. He was dressed badly with cheap jeans and a fleece top. His hair was shoulder length, grey and he had a messy grey beard. She didn't like what she saw but walked over anyway.

'Hi, are you Galston?' she offered her hand out to him.

Galston looked up at her, jolted from his daydream. A young woman was standing next to him, pretty. It was her job to be he thought as he stood up unsmiling and looked her up and down blatantly.

'Aye,' he said sitting down again, she sat opposite and ordered coffee from the steward who had appeared from nowhere.

'Last night?' he asked her.

She nodded. 'Yes, good.'

'Daed ya fuck im?' Galston asked directly. He spat it out. He knew what she did for a living. He didn't really have any opinion either way on prostitution, it was just another means of making money to him. He had no opinion on the legalities of the profession but had strong opinions on prostitutes. He didn't like them. Sabine looked away not answering. The uneasiness she felt after first seeing him was multiplying fast. She had sensed danger as soon as she saw him in the reception and she was rarely wrong. It was vital in her job.

She didn't take every job. She didn't have to. She wasn't greedy so could afford to be picky. She would steer well clear from men like Galston for very good reasons. Right now every alarm bell in her body was jangling, telling her to stand up immediately. Leave. Walk away.

'Ah said, daed ya fuck im?' he asked again more directly.

She looked him directly in the eye and replied, 'Yes.'

She looked towards the barman carrying coffee towards her and then back at Galston. 'Yes, I fucked him.'

Galston nodded at this and seemed to relax a little. 'Coffee's shite,' he said as the barman placed her cup on the small table between them, he frowned.

Was this an attempt to make light conversation, she thought? And then ignored it, she did not relax one bit, her body tight and tense.

'Ya seeing him again?' he asked.

'Tonight.'

'Uhuh,' he was thinking. 'Yur sorted fer Saturday, right?'

'Yes I know what to do.' Sabine's tonality was direct and functional. Not a hint of emotion in her voice. 'Do you?'

Galston looked at the young female sitting in front of him. She was very pretty. Seemed a shame that she was a prostitute. She could easily be any one of the young women he saw in Glasgow. The successful business women, the happily married women. Instead he looked at her sitting in front of him and all he saw was a prostitute. She was different to the skinny, bruised, scratching women he knew but she was a prostitute all the same. She sold her body to men for money, and regardless of how good she looked, Galston didn't like her.

'Dinnae worry love yal get sorted properly,' he said quietly, his mind elsewhere.

Sabine sipped her coffee and hoped this conversation would be over soon. She had a job to do and she would do it but made a mental note to never accept anything like this again. Regardless if it paid double what she would ordinarily get for a weekend job.

Galston checked his watch and then smiled, 'Mon, lets gae up tae ma room.'

Sabine took another sip from her coffee calmly. Replacing the cup slowly she looked him directly in the eye. 'Fuck off.'

Galston laughed. His face changed immediately. It softened and reminded Sabine of her grandfather many years before. He laughed and stood up.

'Aye, right we'll see,' he said, still laughing as he stood. He then left the reception area, heading for the lift leaving Sabine alone.

She sat there and watched him leave. Her chest was tight and she could feel a numbness in her lips from the anxiety. She exhaled slowly but the alarm bells kept ringing. She was very scared. This was a situation she vowed three years ago to never find herself in again. She could leave now, simply check out and disappear but she knew deep down this wasn't the answer. No she would see this through, per the agreement, take the money *then* disappear.

She sipped her coffee and sent an SMS to Craig.

Thirty seconds later Craig clicked on the SMS and smiled from his bed.

Hotel St Anton, 8pm x

He would be there he thought to himself as he luxuriated in his single bed. He felt a familiar happy ache from the night before activities. He could still smell her, taste her. His back stung slightly from her nails, his head pounded but he was smiling.

He replied:

Will be there, with food, what room x

He locked his phone, jumped out of bed still fully clothed and marched through to the living room.

'Guys tonight, no waiting up now,' he said loudly with a smile as he passed Ewan and James in the sitting room on his way to the bathroom. They watched him pass. It was Ewan who spoke, 'You're a twat Craig, know that don't you?'

Craig turned at the door of the bathroom. 'Uhuh' he said and disappeared through the door, locking it behind him. James walked up to the door, he knocked. 'Craig.'

'What?'

'Remember outta here first thing tomorrow?'

'Got it, Jeemac,' the voice said from behind the door. It was muffled as Craig brushed his teeth. James leaned against the door. 'Remember, 7am and we're out of here. Gonna tell me where you will be, just in case?'

Craig opened the door. He was shirtless and had toothpaste around his mouth. 'Ok, Mum. The St Anton. If I'm not here, phone me, if I don't pick up, I'll get home myself.'

He closed the door and James walked back through to the sitting room.

From behind the door Craig shouted. 'Tell Susan fuck all? Tell her I had to meet the bank on Monday ok?' Adding, 'But only if she asks mind?'

'Fine,' James said, shaking his head and sitting down next to Ewan. Ewan looked at him and smiled before returning to his book.

James picked up his phone and typed an SMS of his own, this time replying to one he had received from Scotland.

I had a lot of fun the other night. Want to meet again? x

He re-read it, heard Craig singing in the shower, and clicked the send button.

Chapter 6

Three years ago, at the same time Craig and James were bringing Ewan into Orchid to help with third company, Sabine Weinstrom was living in Heidelberg. She had moved there from Dusseldorf the year before after being accepted into the Universität Heidelberg to study Economics. At twenty-seven she was older than her fellow students but she didn't mind this. University had not been her first choice in life after high school. This decision had initially come as a huge disappointment to her parents. University was never not an option in their view. They had, however, somehow overlooked one very important fact, something they had taught their little princess as she was growing up. She possessed free will. It was on her eighteenth birthday she exercised this free will and announced to her horrified parents she would not be going to university. It took her seven years of working and going nowhere with it to realise that this was a mistake and they were right all along but she was mature enough to admit it to them. Of course this only after she had been accepted. Her mother and father were proud. They didn't tell her so but the fact she made the decision herself – without their pressure – made them even more proud.

She was still young enough to enjoy university life with her fellow students and she would be the first to admit she was having the time of her life. Heidelberg for Sabine was perfect, not too big, not too small. She had managed to secure a small loft apartment in a 17th-century building on Mönschgasse through family connections. From her living room/study/kitchen she could see the ruins of the old castle and was surrounded by the old town. The church bell would chime every fifteen minutes and Sabine absorbed it all. She had grown up in a post-war-built stark concrete suburb of Dusseldorf. History was something she only glimpsed on family weekends away from the city. Every evening she would walk from the university and stop at a café on Karlsplatz to drink a coffee, and watch the tourists and students mingle and socialise.

She was naturally pretty. Her dark black hair fell to her shoulders in a natural loose curl and she had been fortunate to have inherited her mother's understated facial features, nothing standing out. Milky white skin covered a thin frame and the curves were all appropriately proportioned. She was happy with her appearance and, at that juncture, also her life. Student life suited her. The studying, the parties, the infinite possibilities. When she thought back to those times, as she often did now, the sun was mostly shining and it was warm. She was usually wearing one of her thin summer dresses and smiling. Winter hits the medieval town the same as it does everywhere in Germany. Sabine simply chose to remember the summer time or the winter market or the silence of a snow insulated cobbled street. Flakes as big as birds floating gently around her as she walked back to her apartment.

Mostly though it is summer time.

It was during her second semester in the Universität that Sabine started to work occasionally as a prostitute.

She supplemented her allowance and savings by escorting men. A friend jokingly suggested it one evening and the seed was planted. She had some experience in sex. It was limited but she felt she knew what men wanted and over a few weeks managed to persuade herself with a simple 'Why not?' Armed with a basic website she became Sabrina and in doing so also reduced her age to twenty-three.

Normally the men she escorted weren't really very interested in the activities she offered on the website. She would offer to accompany her clients on evenings out, partaking in activities such as fine dining, visits to the theatre or the opera. Of course, the website added, should they find each other mutually attractive then whatever happened between them was something between consenting adults. For such activities Sabine charged her clients €250 per hour. Very few of her clients took her to the opera or dinner. Mostly they wanted to quickly dispense with these activities and fast-forward to the consenting adult part. Sabine, for her part, had never not been attracted to her client once they had settled the paperwork.

Escorting men is a dangerous business and aside from the obvious medical precautions she was very, very, cautious of the men she met. She would carefully scrutinise her clients from a distance before approaching them. Her sense of danger was particularly sensitive, something she inherited from her mother. She would often smile at the five-year-old Sabine and with her finger to her lips tell her, 'It's our little secret.' One time when she was eight years old they both shouted 'stop' at the same little boy who was just about to cross the road. He hesitated and turned to them as a bus came hurtling around the corner too fast. They both continued on to the Rewe supermarket holding hands smiling.

She would always insist on meeting in a public place and would never take a client back to her apartment, preferring to use hotels away from the old town area. She also didn't work that often, one client a week was her average. She didn't need the money that much and contrary to the statement on her website Sabine didn't really enjoy the work.

All in all, it was not an ideal situation but Sabine liked the additional money and knew that it was only temporary until she graduated and started her career in marketing proper.

It never happened though and as Sabine lay on her bed in the Hotel St Anton waiting for Craig she felt the same feeling she did that night two years ago. She had received a call from the American Army base, a young man, on his birthday. She felt the anxiety, her internal warning system starting up but she ignored them as she rode the tram to the base.

She felt the same feeling now and knew she would ignore it,

again.

There was a quiet knock at the door. She jumped off the bed, checked herself in the mirror, fixed a smile on her face, and let Craig into the room.

* * *

Across town James sat in a bar sipping his beer. His laptop was open in front of him but he was looking at his phone, engaged in an SMS conversation with June, his date from the other night. Seems she liked him and James was happily confirming he liked her a lot as well. The reality was he was ok with her. Conversation was hard to drag out but sex was sex and James just figured she was conversationally shy. His saw no reason to tell her the truth, and in any event, it might not be the truth. James would try hard to squeeze the personality out of her and, while he was doing so, he figured, he might as well have fun. It was the most logical approach in his head but he was wise enough to not share these thoughts with her. She might have an altogether different opinion and there was nothing to be gained from being totally honest.

He put his phone down and looked at the photographs filling the screen of his ultrathin Mac. There were approximately fifty thumbnail images, each one showing various construction sites. He clicked one and it filled the screen. A village well was being dug somewhere in the Democratic Republic of Congo. The filename was DRCWell16.jpg. A young boy was grinning into the camera behind the digging equipment. His teeth, perfectly white. A Hollywood smile. The boy was peering around a yellow drill rig as three villagers, stripped to the waist, operated the equipment. Their dark bodies glistened in the equatorial heat. In the background there was a man with a hardhat, short-sleeved shirt and khaki trousers. James peered closer and saw the Orchid symbol on his helmet.

Orchid provided money to various sources. James and Craig

had wondered long and hard about this. They could anonymously deposit large sums to the global charities such as Save the Children but this didn't really satisfy. They wanted a distant but distinctly more hands on involvement. For example it was James and Craig who decided they would place the order for thirty water-well drilling rigs and fund the engineer to accompany them to their point of use. They didn't choose where, but after a lot of research, they chose what. Mosquito nets, a paediatric HIV clinic, well drilling equipment, they had even funded the building of a school and paid for the first five years wages for the teachers. All in all Orchid was a success. A crime definitely, but as he flicked through the various images supplied by Andreas on a memory stick, he felt comfortable that it was as close to victimless as it could be.

His phone vibrated next to him and he picked it up, another SMS, this time from Craig:

Go w/out me tmrrw, bck Mnday. J

As he read it, another message came in from Craig

J

James didn't bother responding. Sometimes Craig's enthusiasm for all things in life became a little too much for him. He loved it and loathed it in equal measure. He turned his attention back to the photographs.

* * *

Two floors above Sabine's room Galston lay on his bed fully clothed and channel-hopped. Most of the channels were in German or Italian but he did have a small choice of English channels – CNN, BBC World and CNBC. He was bored with the regurgitated news on the television. Before the advent of 24-hour news the bulletin was something worth sitting down for he remembered. Now it was a drop in, drop out concept and he found himself getting irritated as he waited for the main headlines to cycle back on. He killed the TV and thought about tomorrow night and Sandy's plan. Overly complicated and dramatic was his opinion. Yes he could do it he had told Sandy but why take the risk? Sandy's mind was made up and not for changing. Galston was simply doing as he was told but wasn't happy. It wasn't the travel, it wasn't the brutality of what he was tasked to do. It was the complexity. Simple is best in his view and he was rarely wrong. That afternoon after meeting Sabine he had gone shopping. Procuring an axe and hacksaw wasn't difficult in a town where almost every house had a log pile propping up the side of the building. He was careful though, buying the axe and saw in one shop. He found another hardware store to purchase the rope and tape.

* * *

Craig watched her walk naked to the bathroom. He commented on her body and she smiled to herself as she entered the small, mirrored room. As she sat down on the toilet she wondered exactly what would happen. She knew with certainty it wouldn't be good. The moment she met Galston she knew it wouldn't be but she also knew she couldn't do anything about it. Self-preservation was the order of the day and she steeled herself, as usual, to come through it unscathed. There was a problem though, a complexity Sabine hadn't encountered in a long time. She was actually starting to like Craig and this concerned her greatly. Normally having little respect for her clients was easy for her. They were paying for sex and regardless how she acted or what she said the reality was she felt nothing but disgust for the men lying on top of her or below her. It was an act, nothing more and she found it very easy to call time on the session and take their money. The Scotsman lying in her bed was different. He wasn't a client, or at least not directly and he was nice. He was a nice guy and he made her laugh. He was unaware of her real job. To him she was Sabine, junior marketing manager for a pharmaceutical company, enjoying a weekend away by herself after a messy break up with her boyfriend. This was a cover story she had perfected over the years. In keeping with the start of many a long relationship, she was just a girl he had met in a bar and was enjoying the intense sexual exploration phase. He was innocent she thought as she wiped herself, flushed the toilet and stood up to appraise herself in the mirror. She looked at the red, flushed skin of her décolletage and realised it had been many years since that had happened. It made her smile and she felt a nervous twinge in her stomach. A thought which she hadn't had since her pre-college days suddenly popped into her mind; does he feel the same?

She unlocked the bathroom and padded back to the bed still smiling and blushing.

* * *

Galston turned, stood up, and left his room, heading for the bar.

* * *

James drained his glass, folded up his laptop, and left to walk the five minutes distance back to the apartment.

* * *

Craig watched Sabine walk to the bed naked. At that moment his mind, his soul and his total being was absorbed by the beautiful German girl. He grabbed her arm and pulled her back on top of him. She was giggling.

* * *

The following morning, 6.45am, Ewan and James were sipping

coffee at the breakfast bar. They had carried out the usual clean up before departure. Emptying the bins, stripping the beds and removing anything from the fridge which wouldn't last untouched for a month. They assumed Craig wouldn't be returning for an overnight stay and packed up the flat accordingly. If he did return, he could remake his bed himself. The next time James planned to come here he planned to take a guest. He had already decided to take June with him so he wanted the place looking reasonably decent. They sipped coffee in silence. It was way too early for conversation. James had gone to bed early the night before, his body unaccustomed to two consecutive ski days had told him to go. Ewan had been out but he seemed ok. At least he is here he thought. Their flight from Zurich wasn't until midday but the drive time from the high Alpine town to the airport was variable. Anything between two and four hours. Better to be early than late was James's approach and without Craig there, he was in charge. It wasn't an official agreement or anything formal, it just was.

'Come on, let's go,' James said, finishing his coffee.

'Shouldn't we give him till seven?'

'Told you, he's not coming, let's go,' was the curt reply.

James rinsed their cups and they left, locking the heavy wooden door behind them and taking the lift to the underground garage. They climbed into the rental car and then pulled out of their parking spot. As they approached, the automatic door started winding up revealing a ramp up to street level. James was driving and he pulled the car to a stop at the top of the ramp. He automatically looked in both directions, even though there was no chance of there being traffic this time of the morning. As he glanced left he saw Craig running down the street. He indicated right and pulled up alongside the curb to wait for him to arrive. Craig reached the car, breathless.

'Thank fuck. Tried calling you!' he said between gasps, leaning against the roof of the car.

'Good morning, Craig,' James said from the driver's seat. 'Changed your mind? Coming home now?'

'Alright Ewan?' Craig said, looking into the back, ignoring the sarcastic question and regaining his composure.

'Craig,' Ewan nodded at him from the back.

'No, haven't changed my mind, don't have a key that's all, left it in there,' he said, smiling.

James shook his head. 'You know, one day this is all going to come crashing down?' Craig just looked at him grinning. He continued, 'One day you are going to get caught and when you do, don't go looking for a bed at my fucking place, ok?'

'Thanks mate.'

James handed him the keys, Craig put them in his pocket and banged on the roof.

'Better get going, only got five hours to drive, what is it? A two-hour drive?' he said with a happy voice.

'See you later and be careful,' James said pressing the window button and pulling away.

* * *

At 6.30am Craig had woken with a start. He had only fallen properly asleep four hours earlier but for some reason his body decided it was a good time to wake up. He stretched his legs under the crisp white sheets and felt her lying next to him. Turning he saw the back of her head, dark hair spread over the pillow and he rubbed his foot up the back of her calf watching her move, still deep in sleep.

He lay there staring at the wooden beams lining the ceiling and let his mind wander. He thought about Susan back in Edinburgh. It was only 5.30am there so she would still be asleep, assuming that Daniel or Nicola hadn't decided otherwise. Daniel the oldest at five still struggled with spending a whole night in his own bed so the picture in his mind changed to Susan and

Daniel in bed. The boy's small body sleeping where daddy normally lay. Nicola would be sound asleep, that he was certain of. Sleeping wasn't her problem. In the three years since she was born he couldn't remember a time when she didn't sleep perfectly, happily, and at the right time. He lay there and thought about his current situation. He rolled over and pressed himself against her. She was warm and he felt the soft rounded contours of her body against his. She felt different to Susan, they always did.

For Craig, guilt never really came into it. James asked him once if he felt guilty and after a long pause he honestly answered with no. He never felt guilty and when he was being honest with himself he wasn't sure why this was. He *should* feel guilty, he *should* have remorse and this led him to the conclusion that guilt, along with monogamy, was a fabrication invented by man. Must be he thought. If not he would feel it along with his desire to not be monogamous. Instead he felt the exact opposite. He read somewhere in some magazine that monogamy is an invention. Human beings are not naturally designed to mate for life and this seemed to fit with his own experience. Marriage is obviously an invention and so, therefore monogamy must be the same. There was a logic in this Craig was certain but he still had a nagging doubt in his mind. The irony was he felt guilty for not feeling guilty. He had no inhibitions about sleeping with as many women as he could, but he felt a guilt that he did and didn't have any remorse about it. Perhaps he would if he was discovered, perhaps that was the issue he wondered. You have only committed a crime when you have been caught. In any event as he told himself on many occasions, life was for living and he fully intended to live his until it stopped. Whenever that happened.

This woman was different though. He knew this already after two nights. He had been captivated by her since they met in the Broken. She was funny, smart, incredibly sexy and made him feel almost superhuman. Totally alive. In moments when she thought he wasn't watching he would catch her staring into space like there was something heavy on her mind. Normally he wouldn't really care so long as it didn't interfere with what they were doing. This time it was different, he really *wanted* to know. He desperately wanted to understand what was going on in her head. The night before he asked her as they lay together in the darkness his face just millimetres away from hers. He could feel her breath mixing with his, the darkness was filled with the afterglow of their lovemaking. Never before had he felt so close to someone, the whole universe for that moment centred on their bed, in a hotel, high in the Alps. It was as if his life up to that point had been reduced to a single moment; now.

'Right now. At this exact moment. In this exact place, where are your thoughts?' he had asked her.

She hesitated for the briefest of moments, then it was gone. He could sense it in the darkness. It was there and then it had disappeared. She took his hand in the darkness and placed it between her legs and then placed her hand between his. Her whispered accented voice and gentle massage removed the thoughts from his head.

'I was thinking if you could manage to do what you just did one more time I might just fall in love with you.'

He lay there in the half-light of morning, remembering the night before, pressing himself into her. He could feel himself stirring again and that's when he really sat up with a jolt. His keys, shit.

He dived out of bed and picked up his mobile phone, it was switched off – he always did that. Shit, checking his watch he started throwing his clothes on, Sabine sat up in bed, bleary eyed, 'What's up?'

'My passport is in the flat, I have no keys and James and Ewan are leaving in,' he paused to look at his watch again, 'shit! Ten minutes.'

He slipped his shoes on barefoot, grabbed his jacket and

rushed out the door.

'Will be back,' he shouted as he ran down the hotel corridor. By the time the hotel room door clicked shut he was bounding out through reception to the surprise of the night porter, sitting quietly reading a book.

Craig ran at full sprint through the town's streets, working his way downhill. He turned on his phone as he ran and tried to ring James. He kept on the road. It was gritted and white with salt. The pavement would be like an ice rink this time of the morning. It was well below zero but he felt warm as he ran. As he turned the corner to their street he saw the hire car nose out of the car park and he increased his run, waving his arms. He watched the car pull out and then pull over. He slowed to a jog. He had made it and his grin returned.

Five minutes later as James pulled away, he watched in his rearview mirror as Craig turned and started walking back up the street. James noticed he hadn't bothered to go towards the apartment. He had just turned around and started back the way he had come, walking this time. At the end of the street, James glanced once more and saw him, this time a small speck, at the other end of the street. James glanced left and right, turned the car and accelerated towards the green highway sign.

He didn't know it then but this was the last time he would ever see Craig alive.

Chapter 7

James sat at his desk staring at the dark window. The pane of glass in front of him reverberated with each gust of wind. The rain hit the window and formed streams which were immediately torn apart by the next gust of wind. Hundreds of droplets the size of marbles crab-crawled their way sideways across the glass, regrouping again in the corner before streaming down and over the window ledge. He sat there staring out into nothing watching their progression. He could hear cars pass by below. The splashes they made as they worked their way along the street, through the puddles. His senses were on high alert. He could taste his lips. He could feel and hear his own heart beating wildly behind his ribs and the cheerful ringtone of his mobile phone was deafening. Almost absently he turned it off and continued staring out at the blackness.

His laptop screen was frozen with the image of Craig tied to a tree.

Galston sat outside in his car. A 99 Mondeo. The rain and wind physically moved the parked vehicle. It rocked side to side with each gust. He had his window half an inch open and blew smoke through the gap. Every so often he felt a splatter of water on his face as it found its way through the gap. He kept his eyes on the flat two levels up. The lights were on and he wondered when James would read the email. He knew that the fat one had read it. Dots had sent him a confirmation message earlier. Apparently he was going "banzai" which was the reaction they expected. Any normal person would lose it. It was a nice place he thought glancing around; the street lights illuminating the old Edinburgh tenement buildings which lined the street. A lighter stone than the red sandstone so common on the west side of the country. It was definitely upscale. Tidy, and the cars parked either side spoke of wealth in these leafy street. The architecture was the same as Galston's childhood. Seven stories high, single entrance, bay windows but this is where the similarity ended he imagined. Here a block would contain eight spacious flats, Galston's would have contained closer to twenty. Sometimes more. He sat and kept his eye on the bay window of the second floor flat. The light was still on but there was no outward sign of anything untoward going on inside. He squeezed the smouldering cigarette butt through the small gap and stretched his feet out. His head hurt, a dull throbbing pain which was the epicentre of a permanent headache. Instinctively he reached up to touch the scar running across his scalp. It was healing but still hurt like hell to touch. The stitches created a red ridge along his hairline. After three weeks it should have stopped hurting but the headaches were getting worse. The number of times Galston had voluntarily seen a doctor could be counted on one finger but after 2pm tomorrow, it would be two. He had booked the appointment earlier today. It wasn't the pain which drove him to go. Sandy had mentioned that there might be a, 'Blood clot or something worse brewing unner yer fuckin ugly head, gae get it seen tae otherwise yer nae use tae me.' So he did.

James stood up and stared around his flat. Everything was the same, clean. But it wasn't the same, everything had changed, everything. Everything was pretend, not real. He hadn't earned any of it. The flat-screen plasma TV hanging on the wall was just a plastic box of cables and tubes. The thick, cream carpet just fibres, nothing more. The dining table, the couch, everything. All a fraud and Craig had died a horror movie death because of it all. And he could go the same way. He walked to the window and placed his hands on the cool glass, his head swimming as he imagined his life slipping away from him. He cried and leaned his face against the glass. He cried for Craig, he cried for the life they had which had now just evaporated and he cried for himself. He cried for what was coming to him.

Galston watched him from below and smiled. He *had* read the email. He waited another five minutes, smoked another cigarette, then climbed out of his car. He retrieved the bottle of wine from the rear seat and turning the collar of his long coat up against the rain he walked, half hunched, towards the tenement entrance.

James locked the door of his flat and slipped his shoes back on. He had no idea where he was going or why he was going out. He just had to get out. He remembered Ewan and turned his phone back on. As he walked down the two flights of stairs his phone picked up a signal and he immediately dialled Ewan's number. He stood in the hallway waiting for the phone to connect, out of the rain. As he waited he looked around and through the glass strip on the door he saw Galston standing outside. He was smiling at him.

Galston knocked on the glass strip of the door. 'Gonna let us in would ya?'

James looked at the grey-haired old man standing in the rain. 'You live here?' Ewan had just answered the phone. 'Hang on Ewan,' he said into the handset. 'Do you live here?' he repeated. This was the last thing he needed right now; normality.

Galston peered through the glass. 'Naw ah don't, visiting someone.' He held up a bottle of wine as he spoke. 'They're nae answering, is pishing down out here man, mon lemmy in would ya?'

James peered out and then opened the door to let the man in. He turned slightly to the side to let the man pass into the hallway and then moved towards the open door.

'Ewan, hang on.' He managed to say before his forward momentum was violently reversed. James felt himself being dragged backwards into the hallway, his feet barely managing to backtrack fast enough. He was stumbling and falling backwards. He was spun around and rammed against the wall. His head battered against the hard tiles and the phone fell from his hand, clattering on the floor. Galston stood in front of him, both hands firmly on his shoulders pushing him into the wall.

'Know who ah am?' Galston spoke directly to his face. Their noses were almost touching. James could smell stale cigarettes and feel the warmth of his breath as he spoke. He shook his head and Galston punched him. Not too hard, but hard enough to start his nose bleeding. 'Best y'start thinking quick sticks cowboy, fuckin know who ah am?' he repeated. He didn't shout. His voice was level and direct.

James was barely able to speak. Panic swept through him and he struggled to form words. His lips shook uncontrollably. 'I think so,' was all he could manage in response.

'Aye, course ya dae. There ya gae,' he patted him on the shoulders. 'Now calm the fuck down. You'll be shiteing yerself maer if ya keep acting like a dick ok?'

James nodded.

'Ya really need tae get this, dae exactly what ah say and fuck all I'll happen.'

James just stared at him.

'Get it?' He pulled him back and slammed him against the wall again.

James nodded quickly.

'Wir gonna walk oot a here now. An we're. That's you and me, we're gonna have a wee chat, ok?' He paused staring at James still holding his shoulders pressed against the hard-tiled wall. 'Nae fannying around. Dunna gae daein anything daft mind.'

James nodded again. Blood was running freely down his face now. It was warm. His heart rate was slowing and he could start to feel a sense of control returning to his body. He tried to take stock of the situation but whichever way he looked it was grim.

Galston released his grip. He bent down and picked up his phone and the bottle of wine which had miraculously survived being dropped onto the hard-tiled floor. Galston studied the phone. It was still connected to Ewan, he hung up. He passed it back to James, 'That'll be you'. He then turned back towards the security door. 'Mon,' he said as he pulled the door open and turned to James.

James ran.

It wasn't a conscious decision. In the second it took Galston to open the door his body was decided, even if his mind wasn't. He didn't weigh up the pros and cons of such an action. He didn't calculate the chances of being caught or the likelihood of tripping or finding the back door locked. He just ran.

He ran down the stairs and out into the shared grass courtyard behind the flats. He ran fast into the darkness, full speed. His slip on shoes slid on the dark grass and mud and he fell almost immediately. His knees landing in the soft earth and his right elbow jarring against something hard. He imagined Galston directly behind him as he picked himself up. He started running again, his feet slipping as he panicked. He ran directly across the grass towards the faint light of the close opposite. He gathered momentum and in the darkness ran straight into one of three rotary clothes dryer set up in the shared space. His face and torso connected directly with the pole and he fell backwards onto the muddy grass. He couldn't breathe. The wind had been knocked out of him and he felt dazed. He was wild with panic now and scrabbled to stand up again. His fingers clawed at the muddy sodden grass until he felt purchase, and then he ran again. This time he reached the close. He ran inside and stopped. His breathing was hard and fast. The adrenaline flooding his body kept him on extreme high alert. Inside it was dark and quiet. He looked back but couldn't see anything. He started again, taking the stairs in two strides and burst out onto the street running parallel to his own. He ran down the street to the corner and turned right, up the hill. At the top was the park and beyond that a rabbit warren council estate. As he reached the park his run slowed to his more familiar jog. His knees, elbow and face ached. He was soaked through. His dress shoes heavy with sodden mud. He slowed to a walk once inside the park.

Branches and other storm debris littered the football pitch and he picked his way through this, glancing backwards every couple of seconds.

Galston stood in the close after he left for a few minutes. He stood there deciding what to do. He wasn't going to chase the stupid cunt. He couldn't and in any case where was he going to go? He looked around and then walked up the steps towards James's flat. The door was on the right-hand side of the stairwell. A hessian mat and some running shoes sat outside. Galston checked the name plate and then walked over to the flat opposite. The door was of wood with the centre section made up of stained glass. An Indian girl with full headdress in green and blue stared out at him with lifeless glass eyes. He stood very still for a minute, listening. Other than the sound of the storm outside it was just another quiet early evening. A television could be heard from the floor above and there was a distant sound of a baby crying. He walked back to James's flat and tried the door. Locked. He pushed it hard and the door warped around a single point, the Yale lock just below the handle. It was a new door, not original like the flat opposite. He pushed again, harder this time and the door warped more but the lock was not moving at all. It was solid. He sighed, stepped back and aimed a single kick hard dead centre against the lock. It gave and door flew open banging against the wall, wood splinters showered the carpeted hall and he kicked them away as he stepped into the flat.

James walked randomly through the estate. The weather meant he was alone on the streets as he zigzagged away from his flat. He walked for twenty minutes before convincing himself he was safely out of reach. Only then did his thoughts return to what to do. He kept walking and started to make some phone calls.

Chapter 8

July 2005. Tony Parr sat in the control room and watched the bank of monitors. Black-and-white feeds to London's maze of tunnels and passageways which made up the world's oldest underground system. With over 400km of track there was a lot to cover but fortunately today Tony was only interested in one station. This particular control room covered the Northern, City and Central lines but for now all monitors were set to Stockwell station. In all, eight monitors covered pretty much every public area in the station. A team of four young men dressed in civilian clothing filled the room, each taking two screens, each with an earpiece. The control-room manager paced behind them nervously. The men were armed, hair cut short and had zero sense of humour. He had received the call an hour before they came, a simple 'give them the access they need', no other information. He did as he was told but wasn't happy about it.

Tony sat quietly watching the sea of people flood into the underground station. It was 10am. Each face was a blur but Tony saw everyone. He didn't speak, barely blinked, just scanned from face to face as they flowed across the screen. It was hypnotic.

He heard him before he saw him, the man to his right monitoring the Clapham Road approach alerted them. 'Target approaching the station.'

'Pass on the description and have them confirm ID,' Tony said without moving his eyes from the screen. He heard the description being passed down the line and watched as the suspect entered the station. Dark brown jacket, jeans, rucksack, dark skin. Tony watched him appear at the top of the screen and then disappear at the bottom.

'I've lost him,' he said and stood up moving to the screens to his right. He watched as their target walked to the barrier and placed his wallet on the oyster card reader. The man moved through the barriers and turned right for the north bound Northern line.

'Have they got him?' he asked the blond-haired man sat in front of him.

'Yes, there they go,' the agent said pointing to the screen as three men followed the suspect through the barriers.

'Did they ID him?'

'Yes positive, they stood behind him at the barrier, I confirmed.'

'Good. Well gentlemen our work here is done.' Tony stood up and looked at the control-room manager. 'Cheers mate,' he said with a smile and picked up his leather jacket. 'Queen and country and all that shit.'

They left the room en masse.

As they worked their way out of the ugly concrete building housing the control room Tony continued to listen in on the operation. Their job was done, reconnaissance only. They had been following and monitoring the suspect for three months by that point and had chosen the day and time to put a halt to his Al-Qaeda shenanigans. The trick was to balance the burden of proof, a smoking gun, without the suspect actually firing it in the first place. In Ankif's case the bomb-making equipment would be sufficient to sway any jury in their favour. He had taken delivery yesterday evening and Tony decided to put an end to it this morning, Monday 22nd July. Tony's simple conclusion was it wouldn't be much fun having a rag-head radical on the loose in the city with all the constituent parts to take out a building or two. His official report on the operation said as much. He just worded it differently.

They exited the stairwell and Tony looked across the road at the Tube station. Cars, buses and taxis filled the street. He looked around. A normal day in a normal London Borough. He could hear the ongoing operation deep beneath the busy street and was mentally visualising their progress. Two officers were already on the platform. The plan was to grab the guy as soon as he reached the platform. Right next to the stairs there was an office, a disused office. Inside a further two officers waited. The plan was to bundle him in there, clear the area, and then get him the fuck out. The rucksack was a worry for all concerned but the chances of the target actually making a working device overnight were zero. But it did add an extra dimension to the operation. Everyone was twitchy, their edgy voices said as much. The Met made the call to continue with the deep underground take. In simple terms, in the choice of nightmare scenarios they chose the bomb underground rather than out in the open in a busy London street. And for once Tony agreed with them.

He was approaching the final stairs. The two officers confirmed they were in place. It would be smooth, Tony knew this. The target was confined underground, three officers tailing him as he walked down towards a full on welcoming party.

'Hang on,' a voice urgently broke over the static. Tony froze mid-stride.

'More people coming.'

'Where from?'

'Fuck, there are loads of them!'

'Do you still have eyes on the target?'

Silence.

'DO YOU STILL HAVE THE TARGET?'

'Yes,' came the worried response.

Tony turned and stood gazing into the window of a newsagent opposite the Tube station entrance. He was listening intently now, his team were doing the same at different places along the street.

'Yes, still have target, he's approaching you now. Confirm sighting?'

'Confirmed.'

Silence.

'I think he's seen us, he's stopped. He's staring straight at us, shit.'

'He's running, fuck!'

Tony turned and ran directly across the street. His team followed. Traffic swerved and horns blared. He ran straight into the station entrance and vaulted the barriers followed by three other men all dressed similarly. The voices in his ear were relaying what was rapidly becoming a catastrophic fuck up deep below.

'He's on the train. Wait, yes I see him. It's him, he's on the train,' the voice sounded young and scared.

'I'm going to approach him...'

'Wait!' another voice broke in.

'He's seen me. I'm on the train. He's seen me, fuck.'

'Ankif, stay where you are. I am an armed police officer. Do not move. DO YOU UNDERSTAND ME?'

There was silence in Tony's earpiece; he sprinted down the escalators, taking the steps three at a time. People squeezed themselves to the side to allow the group access.

Tony heard the gunshots in the earpiece and their echo running up through the tiled passageway. It sounded like three rounds had been fired but the echo could have multiplied that. He kept running, his shoes slapping against the polished floor. Someone was screaming.

'Suspect down, suspect down,' the young voice confirmed.

'Confirmed suspect down,' another calmer voice said.

Tony slowed at the top of the stairs and jogged the final few steps, removing his ID as he did so. The train was at the platform. People were lying on the floor. One of the carriage windows had shattered. Tony approached slowly, hands at his side. He showed his ID to one of the Met officers at the sliding door.

'What happened? I was on the recon team.'

'He went for his rucksack. We took him down. Not much else to say really. The fuck else could we have done?'

Tony nodded and walked through the carriage. A young

Japanese couple sat looking scared. They watched him. He approached the body and nodded to the young police officer trying to look in the bag without touching it. No older than twenty-five Tony thought. He saw books and an MP3 player in the half open bag.

He looked into the face of the young man lying on the train floor. It took him a second to realise but once he did he looked around, stood up, and walked off the train.

'Good luck,' he said to the older officer at the door as he passed.

'Wha..?'

'You killed the wrong fucking man.'

Tony slowly walked up and out of the station eventually emerging into the daylight. This was the start of the end of his military career.

Five years later just outside of Livingston he sat watching television in his semi-detached non-descript house. He never really thought about his military days now. It used to piss him off. It wasn't his fault the Met had lost the target on the stairs that day. He had done his job and it certainly wasn't his fault Jean Charles de Meneze was shot. It turned out Meneze had overstayed his student visa and thought the police were following him for that. His mistake was to look similar to the real target, act nervous, to have a rucksack and to run. None of these individually should be a death sentence but doing all three in the wrong place and at the wrong time turned out to be one for Meneze. Tony didn't even blame the officer who shot the guy. He probably would have done exactly the same. It was just a tragic, and ultimately a career-limiting set of circumstances.

The general public didn't see it in such a forgiving light though. The headlines made sure of this and Tony was one of three who had been asked to leave, quietly. Don't complain – you get the full pension. Complain – we throw the book at you. This was how it worked, he understood this no matter how much it pissed him off. He left quietly and did what most men with his very specific training did. He started his own security company.

He sat and watched a daily magazine show, the sort which took little concentration and provided background noise and colour. He ate his dinner, lasagne, from its cardboard, oven-proof container and watched them discuss cooking with flowers. They are edible and tasty the presenter told the audience before eating a blue/grey one in its entirety with a theatrical flourish. He munched and made appreciative noises as he did so. Sure, Tony thought, as he struggled to eat the layers of pasta and mince without burning his mouth. It was straight from the oven. He sat on his couch and crouched over his coffee table picking around the edges of the scalding hot slab of food as the show quickly progressed onto heroic war dogs.

His mobile phone rang. He looked up and ignored it, shovelling another mouthful of the serves two portion into his single mouth.

Tony was large. Not fat, just large. He stood 6ft 2in tall and weighed, the last time he checked, 16 stone. His Italian roots had been diluted four times over but he still retained the dark skin, hair and pointed facial features. He didn't care too much for dieting but his four times a week in the gym and football twice a week kept everything in check – for now. Eating a lot at every sitting was something deeply ingrained within him. Eat a lot and eat it fast. He learned this day one of Infantry training at Catterick and twenty years later he still dined in this fashion much to Melissa's distaste. He scraped the cheese melted to the cardboard box with his knife and watched as the show closed out with a colliery brass band marching through the studio.

The phone rang again and he swore out loud in its direction as he put his heavy legs up on the coffee table and took another drink from the beer can. Whoever it is can fucking wait.

Tony met Craig through the football. Every Monday evening they would meet at the local Astroturf pitches and spend two hours kicking lumps out of each other and the other twenty men. Tony joined after a client mentioned it and he had been going religiously for the past three years. Rain, snow, sun, it didn't really matter. He would turn up and take up his usual position as the centre half. His size and speed was a frightening proposition. He would gather the defence around him and bark orders in his thick cockney accent and generally people would listen to him. Of course the pub always followed Monday night football and it was Craig who joined up the dots in his story one evening and came up with a business proposition. He sat there sipping a pint of orange & lemonade and happily talked about his background. He missed out certain parts but in general it was fairly truthful representation and a linear one. School, Army, wife, kids. After being kicked out of school the infantry was one option on a very short list of options. He joined up aged sixteen and for the next fifteen years the army was his life until he was asked to leave five years ago. Craig then talked him through his proposition.

He drained the can, ran his hand through his jet-black hair, and switched the television off. A daily soap opera had just started so he went to find out who was trying to call him.

* * *

James sat on a tree stump and tried the number again. He willed Tony to pick up, come on, answer the fucking thing.

* * *

Tony looked at the phone. It was James. He clicked the green button.

Tony usually measured his life in stages; before the Army, the Army and after the Army. He didn't know it yet but in thirty seconds he would be adding a new one. Before and after Craig died.

'James?' he said.

* * *

Galston sat back on the couch and looked around. The living room was decorated plainly but with taste. Two, two-seater brown leather couches sat at right angles, a small table sat in the bay window. The colours were plain, cream and light brown carpet. He glanced back and saw the muddy footprints on the otherwise spotless flooring. A large TV on the wall with no obvious sign of cables. Even Galston could appreciate it. It was nice and looked expensive. The kettle popped and he went to finish making himself a cup of tea. He might even stay the night. He had already 'fixed' the door. Stuck the splintered wood back in place on the outside with Blu-tac and closed the door. Unless someone studied the door closely nothing would appear untoward. The only person who might study it in detail would be James and he was reasonably sure he wasn't going to return anytime soon. Returning to the living room with his cup of tea, he turned the TV on and settled back on the couch. He liked it here he thought as he absentmindedly ran his fingers across the scar. A soap opera had just started.

* * *

'Tony...thank fuck.'

'What's going on?' Tony asked.

James stood looking out over the park – a green respite from the urban claustrophobia. Branches and sodden rubbish lay everywhere, storm debris. Tonight it just looked forlorn.

'Craig was murdered,' he said.

Tony stood in his kitchen with the phone to his ear, he was not prepared for the message he had just heard.

'How?' he asked. It seemed the most logical place to start.

James walked Tony through the last two hours. It took about ten minutes including questions.

Tony had screwed up and now someone was dead. James didn't say it but Tony said it to himself. His job was to make sure it never even came close to this.

'You spoken to Ewan?'

'Yes, he got the email as well.'

'Where is he now?'

'Home, I think.'

Tony's brain kicked into the "do something" mode. In the Army it was the equivalent of dealing with the three mad Afghanis running directly at him before worrying about the other ten thousand waiting just over the hill. Secure the immediate vicinity first – and he started doing exactly that.

'Ok, listen to me. Once you hang up here, remove the battery from your phone, it's probably nothing, but from now on we are not taking any chances, ok?'

'Ok.'

'No, before you do that,' he corrected himself, 'phone Ewan and tell him to meet you somewhere. Get together the two of you and tell him to do the same with his phone, ok?'

'Ok.'

'I'll pick you both up at the bus stop across from Haymarket station at 9.30pm. Be there. The two of you.'

'Ok.'

'Ok good. Now go get Ewan.'

Tony pressed the red button on his phone. Fuck, this is bad, really bad. Craig's dead. Tortured and killed, fuck, fuck, fuck. Why didn't he see this coming? His brain was slowly splitting up the various pieces of information and automatically working out what to do. First things first. Make sure Ewan and James are safe. Second, make sure Susan and Sarah and the kids are also safe. He instantly realised it was an impossible task to hide and protect that many people. Plan A had become plan B already.

In times of crisis he preferred to act. Without a firm plan he just did the next thing on the obvious list. He left his house and started the drive towards the city.

Thank God Melissa was out.

* * *

Ten minutes later across the city Ewan was packing a bag, a small rucksack. He had removed the battery from his mobile phone as instructed. A change of clothes and some toiletries. James had asked for clothes but he had nothing which would fit. He threw a one-size-fits-all anorak in the bag. When he was done he sat down on his couch and stared at the wall. Craig was dead and it was certain it was his fault. He stared at the wall and willed himself to cry. Any normal person would cry. But instead he just felt guilty. The guilt had been building up since they came knocking on his door but he believed Tony had fixed it; an elegant solution to his and their problem. No reason to say anything. It had gone away, right? He stared at the wall and for once didn't know what to do. He wanted to drink, that's what he wanted to do. His hands started shaking when the thought entered his head so he walked to the bookshelf, poured himself an inch of whisky and emptied it in one gulp. The liquid burned, he savoured the sensation and then filled the glass again. Walking round the flat he checked every room. It suddenly didn't feel safe inside so he downed the second measure and left the flat. In all twelve minutes had passed since James had phoned.

Outside Dots saw the lights go out and sat up in his car. He had been sitting there three hours and his legs were stiff. He wiped the condensation from the windscreen and watched the main door of the block through the streaked gap. Within thirty seconds it was open and Ewan started walking down the street towards him.

Ewan walked stooped, the rucksack over one shoulder. The rain was heavy and he pulled the hood on his jacket up. He did so as he passed Dots in the car. He was on the phone and Ewan failed to notice him.

'Fat boy's walking?' he asked Galston on the other end of the line.

'Ok?'

Dots paused. 'Gonna let me know what ya want me tae dae, Gal, eh?'

'Fucksake, gotta brain ave you? Follow him.'

'Right.'

'Walk, he might jump oan the bus, you'll lose him.'

'Is fuckin pishing down, Gal.'

'Walk.' He hung up and stretched out on the couch.

Dots climbed out of the car into the storm. He was wearing a thin jacket which was instantly soaked through. He followed Ewan from a distance of about one hundred meters. When he turned the corner he ran, waited at the corner, watching before trailing him again. It was a maze of streets here and there was a real risk of losing his target.

* * *

James shuffled out onto the main street. Traffic was light but there were still people around. An Indian take-away seemed to be doing a roaring trade. The bus stop was around the corner from the take-away, on a quieter street. He hurried past the people. He was a mess. His hair matted to his head, mud coated his dress trousers and his shoes were sodden. He knew his face was covered in dried blood. He walked fast head down, past the takeaway and around the corner. He made it to the bus shelter and stepped back into the gorse bush which lined the scrub land behind it. It smelled of piss and dog shit but James ignored this and shuffled further into the undergrowth to wait.

* * *

Fifteen minutes later Ewan turned into the street and walked past the takeaway. He turned the corner and then looked around to see if anyone was following him. It was a futile act but made him feel better. He just saw lots of people and cars, anyone of which could be following him. He continued to the shelter and stood under the graffiti covered plastic shelter to wait for James.

'Right, he's headin tae the bus,' Dots said from the corner of the street. He could see the fat one standing under the shelter.

'Where they headin?'

'Haven't a Scooby.'

'Get oan it then,' Galston instructed. He was quite enjoying this from the warmth of James's flat. He'd found the whisky cabinet and had already decided to stay the night.

'Sure?'

'Just catch the fuckin—'

'Wait!' Dots interrupted him. 'Ya fuckin dancer, oer ones here. Walked oot of the bushes.'

'Great.' Galston laughed at this, imagining how James must look by now. 'Get the bus, find oot where they're off tae.'

Dots pressed himself against the wall to avoid the rain. 'Is pure Baltic out here man, can ah nae drive?'

'Get yersel oan the fuckin bus.' Galston hung up and sipped a 35-year-old MaCallen. He was smiling.

* * *

Ewan turned and physically jumped, he wasn't expecting James to creep up on him. 'Jesus Christ, what the hell happened to you?'

'Met the guy who did Craig in.'

'Christ, James, this is bad, this is totally fucked up you know?' James just nodded.

'How bad do I look?' he asked.

'Like shit. Hang on.' He took a sock from his rucksack and wet it in a puddle.

'Give your face a wipe, get the blood off,' he said, passing the sock to James.

'Going to meet Tony right?' he asked as his friend tried to get the worst of the blood off. He took the anorak from his bag as well. James nodded.

'Put this on, put the hood up, it'll hide most.'

'Thanks, what about now?' he asked, indicating to his face. Ewan took the sock to help him.

'You been drinking?' James asked him, smelling his breath as his friend wiped the remaining blood stuck to his face.

'Of course I've fucking been drinking,' he replied, rubbing James's chin. 'Where we off to?'

'Haymarket.'

Chapter 9

By the time Craig returned to the room Sabine had showered. She hadn't dressed but felt a lot better washing away the residue from the night before. She heard the key card in the door and lay down on top of the covers naked. The smile on her face was genuine.

'Where've you been?' she asked in an over-the-top made-up husky voice, moving her legs a little on the bed.

Craig looked at her and started to undress. His smile was also genuine.

'Just out,' he said moving to the bed kicking his jeans off. He stood there naked in front of her. 'But I'm back now.'

They emerged from the room at midday to eat and walk. The sun actually felt warm even though the temperature barely reached freezing at its warmest. They walked through the town chatting. Craig avoided mentioning the fact that he was married with two children and Sabine, for her part, managed to avoid mentioning that she was a prostitute paid to set him up. Even if the odds were stacked against them actually having a real relationship they each found themselves being sucked into the fabrication. The relationship could be real they told themselves and each inwardly tried to figure out how to make it so. It had to be real, Craig thought. He had already run the various scenarios through in his head, Susan, the kids, the fallout. But at that point he had already made his mind up.

Sabine had to deliver him at a specific time and place. This was her job. She didn't actually know why but the alarm bells were ringing every time she thought of it. Whatever it was it couldn't be good. They had approached her through her website and it was put to her that this was a surprise for Craig. A good surprise, a nice surprise, a 21st birthday or stag party surprise she had assumed. After meeting Galston it was very clear there was nothing good about this surprise. The question in her mind now wasn't whether it would be bad or good. It was just how bad would it be? She had worked this over in her head and concluded Craig couldn't be everything he said he was but this was hardly something she could hold against him coming from her. She figured he was on the run, hiding from this man Galston who needed to find him. They would talk and that would be that. They might fight, but whatever the problem Craig had – it could be resolved, couldn't it? And Sabine was determined to be there when it was. She had made her mind up to gamble on the Scotsman, a man she didn't even know existed until last night.

They walked and chatted, drank coffee and then made their way back to the room. They still had a few hours before dinner and they both knew how they wanted to spend those precious hours.

At 8pm Sabine had to make sure Craig was in a particular spot.

As soon as they were inside the room she kissed him deeply. His tongue darted into her mouth and she could feel his hands pulling her shirt out of her jeans. She held his face between her hands as he undressed her, the anticipation was electric but she still couldn't rid herself of the sense of foreboding. In the last two days she had felt something strong. It had been a long time since she had felt anything. She wanted him to undress her. She wanted to feel his urgency and she really wanted to spend time with him. She forced herself to compartmentalise everything and focus on Craig as he pushed her jeans down to her knees.

* * *

Two floors above them Galston lay on his bed. He was bored. He had walked around the town three times, drank coffee and had eaten some lunch. The clean air, the sun-bleached wooden buildings and the alpine views which had initially overwhelmed him were now just boring. He had had enough of this other world and was looking forward to getting it done and getting the fuck back to what he knew. He lay on his bed and stared at the wooden beamed ceiling. CNN played quietly in the corner. As he did more and more frequently recently, his mind drifted back over his life. He did have plans but in retrospect it was clear that planning and mapping out the future was a waste of time. Life is about events. Actions and reactions. You can plan as much as you like. It won't happen. Whatever you plan will be fucked up by something or someone. Craig is going to learn that. Tam learned it and he had learned it. It was going to be St Mirren then Rangers and perhaps Scotland, Hampden and the glory for Tam. They had mapped it out together. Then it was fucked up by the combination of a balmy summer's evening, four young men with too much testosterone and a healthy dose of the Scottish-hard-man disease – booze. Galston had lain there and watched the life ooze out of his friends ears and heard the laughter as their attackers staggered away. He lay there and started to map out what would happen next.

It took him some weeks to recover. He spent a week in the Royal Infirmary during which time he had been interviewed twice by the police. They would do fuck all though. They spent a lot of time on the question of why? Why did they kill him? Why did they start on the two of you? What did you do to provoke them? Galston kept his mouth shut. No point in helping them, it was just another street killing in a city bursting at the seams with street crime. A young man beaten to death in a rough area. This was hardly headline news. Motive? They had no motive you stupid cunt, don't you realise that? They were pissed and they wanted to do it. For a laugh, good enough motive for you? Because they were bored? It was irrelevant really. Tam was dead for no good reason and Galston spent the week planning.

He knew exactly who three of them were.

Two of them were brothers, Billy and James McNally. They worked a different shift to him at Goodyear, he would see them at the changeover. Laughing and joking. Fucking around. They were twenty-five and twenty-seven years old respectively so that put them ten years older than himself. He knew one of the other two, Brian Cox. He didn't know where he worked but knew of him by his reputation. He was seen as a bit of a ladies man, dark hair, muscular and good-looking. Galston remembered it was Brian who had jumped on Tam's head. He had stood up on a bench and looked down at Tam as he lay in the foetal position protecting himself from the kicks. He laughed as he launched himself, two-footed, from the bench. Galston could see his face in his mind. He had a lopsided smile, an evil smile.

He had seen the fourth man but he couldn't put it together, he saw him but he didn't, he was just out of reach of his memory. Galston ignored him for now and focused on the other three.

He lay on the bed and even though these events occurred over forty years ago the memory still made him wince. In the intervening years he had witnessed a lot of violence and death but none which made him react so strongly.

Billy McNally was a pisshead.

He would drink at every available opportunity. Weekdays and sometimes even on shift he would drink. He drank to get drunk. It was far from a social thing for Billy. He drank because he wanted to get drunk nothing else. It didn't really matter if he had company or not. Invariably with Billy after the booze came the violence. He would erupt into a frenzy of violence at the slightest thing and in this city the slightest thing was a common occurrence. It didn't matter who it was or whether it was male or female, young or old. He would lash out punching, kicking, using anything which came to hand – a glass, a pipe, a brick. One night he pounded a priest's face to pulp using a heavy-bound leather bible. It really didn't matter much to Billy. He had quite a few nasty looking scars on his pale grey face from these drunken adventures. Not everyone he attacked ran away or lay down. The booze was also taking its toll. His face was bloated and even though he was only twenty-five years old the signs of permanent liver damage were there, plain to see.

Galston knew where Billy went to drink and one Saturday evening in August that year he followed him to McGillies bar next to Central Station. It was 6pm when he arrived, so he left to walk around the city knowing Billy would be there a while. He stopped for coffee in Mandeni's coffee bar and listened to the rock and roll music on the jukebox. The city was alive, it was Saturday night and still warm for the time of year. Girls and boys hung around drinking and dancing. It was the height of flower power but Mandeni's still clung defiantly to the rock n' roll era which had expired ten years earlier. He hung around till 9pm and then headed back to the Horseshoe to check on Billy. Peering inside he saw him standing at the bar with a dram and a half. It would still be some time before he was kicked out or he ran out of money. He retreated to the main entrance of the train station and waited. Crowds of people walked past him, mostly dressed for a night out. Groups of girls giggling heading down to the Barrowlands and groups of interested young men following them. Galston stood there, smoking and watching the bar. It was an hour later, just after 10pm when Billy exited. The saloon doors swung open and Billy staggered out onto the street. He steadied himself with his hand on the wall and then regaining his balance started off in the direction of Argyle Street. Galston stubbed his cigarette out and followed him. He knew roughly the route he would take.

Progress was slow but eventually they had cleared the busy streets of central Glasgow and were now picking their way around the half-constructed M8 Clyde crossing. It was where he had grown up but looking around at the building works he struggled to recognise anything. It was just a building site. The only constant was the river, dark and ominous to his left. The river never changed.

Billy was about a hundred yards ahead of him when he turned

abruptly to his left and walked behind one of the temporary Portakabins setup for the workmen. Galston ran to the cabin, paused and then followed him around the back. He was standing there just behind the cabin. One arm steadying himself as he urinated. He was looking down watching the piss puddle form and run in a thick stream between his legs. His legs were spread as if being frisked by the police in one of those American cop shows. Galston kept walking towards him and pushed him hard on the back. Billy hit the cabin wall and fell to his knees in the piss puddle he had just created. He looked around with a drunken look of surprise on his face.

'Fuch ya doin man?'

Galston didn't respond. Billy started to stand up.

'Wha ya doin, ya fuchin nutter?' he asked again as he stood.

Galston hit him hard on the side of the face as he rose and his head banged hard against the prefabricated plywood wall. The wood cracked and he bounced off it, landing with his face in the sand. This time he started moving faster, his mind, dulled by the booze had realised what was occurring. And it wasn't an unfamiliar situation for Billy. He managed to get onto all fours before a foot cracked into his chest breaking four ribs and winding him. Galston stood there and waited for him to move again.

He didn't, instead he started throwing up brown liquid. 'For fuchssake man, wha ya doin is fer?' he gasped between retches. He was scared and his voice was trembling.

'Ahm gonna kill ya. Want ya tae really know it. Yur gonna fuckin die now but ah want you tae know it first. Yur gonna fuckin die an ahm gonna fuckin dae it.' Galston spoke with a venom which surprised even himself. He waited for a response but he got none. Billy was breathing heavy and retching. Brown puke and piss gathered around his knees, the smell of acid ale filled Galston's nostrils. Galston kicked him hard again in the same spot on his chest trying to get a response. He got one, Billy started screaming. The noise was loud in the muffled surroundings so Galston speeded up. He had hoped to slowly torture him. He wanted to play with him. This was how he had played it out in his mind from his bed in the Royal Infirmary. Instead he just repeatedly kicked his head and chest until Billy lay still, on his back. All around blood clotted with sand forming puddles and small red sand marbles. Billy's bloody clothes were soaked with his own urine and vomit. Galston's foot throbbed hard as he caught his breath. He looked around for something to finish it off and found a short scaffold bar. With the bar Galston made sure Billy wasn't getting up again, crashing it into his face repeatedly. When it started to feel spongy he stopped and crouched down to peer into the face which was now just a mush of flesh and bone. He could only make out one eye, the other had disappeared.

He had dreamed and fantasised about this moment ever since the night in July. He pictured it in his head and thought about how elated he would feel. Instead he felt nothing. Nothing at all so he just left him there and walked down to the riverside. Dropping the scaffold bar into the inky waters he walked west. His mind was already mulling over Billy's older brother.

There was a knock at the door of his hotel room and he stood up to open the door. A young man stood there dressed in an ill-fitting, creased suit. Roman was his name according to the lopsided name badge. He spoke with a Slavic accent, 'Sir, would you be having dinner in the hotel tonight. We have a private function on in the main restaurant so just want to inform you of the alternatives.'

'Naw, won't be.' Galston shook his head and closed the door before Roman could say anything else. He walked back into the room and started to unpack his clothes for this evening. He had picked up the ski gear in TK Maxx, cheapest they had on offer for his size and he carefully laid them out on the bed. Once done he looked around, ready to go. He then sat down again. CNN world report had just started, the rise of the Brazilian economy, he clicked the mute button, stood up and walked to the balcony lighting a cigarette as he did so. He still had four hours to kill.

* * *

Craig lay down on top of Sabine and buried his face into her dark hair. He kissed the back of her neck and moved himself gently, slowly, inside her. His breathing was slowing down and could feel her move below him, her breathing was shallow and he rolled off to the side. Holding her body tight to his he curled his legs into hers and wrapped his arm around and over her breasts. They didn't speak for at least five minutes. They savoured the moment. Savoured the feeling.

Eventually she spoke. 'I have booked dinner for tonight, 7pm, hope that's ok?'

'Uhuh,' he said absently into the back of her head, adding, 'I'm not hungry.'

'Yet.'

'No, not yet,' he said with a smile.

Eventually they left the room. The bubble they had created was gossamer thin and they both knew the world outside, whilst not pushing in, needed access to some of their time. As they walked through the reception hand in hand Craig felt strangely detached from the reality outside of their room. Twenty minutes earlier he had been showering with her, washing her naked body and being washed in return. He needed to interact with other people. The concierge, the receptionist, the taxi driver to allow the world in. It wasn't going to go away and tomorrow it would come rushing back whether he liked it or not.

* * *

James and Ewan stood in the bus shelter across from Haymarket railway station.

The wind had died down which allowed the rain to fall vertically for the first time in almost a week. It played a loud tattoo on the plastic roof. They stood there and waited. James was soaked through and wearing the oversized anorak from Ewan. The hood was drawn around his face. He was effectively hiding. Ewan paced up and down nervously. He swore every so often and sometimes kicked rubbish out into the main road. Each kick accompanied by another curse. Cars and taxis hurried by and every so often a bus would slow down but not stop. Neither of them indicated they wanted picking up so the bus changed gear and pulled away. They didn't speak.

* * *

Across the road outside the main railway station Dots stood and smoked. He had followed them on the number 47 bus to the station, boarding at the next stop down. This was the first time he had been asked to follow someone but had watched enough TV and films to understand the basics. Don't be seen staring. Don't be too obvious and, above all, make sure you don't lose them. It appeared simple on screen but the reality on a dreich night like tonight was very different to how he had perceived it. So far so good though he thought as he dialled Galston's number.

'Bodie, this is Doyle. Still have their tail. Still pish wet through. Bawsacks drippin. Over,' he said as soon as it was answered.

'Aye, and?' There was no humour in the response.

'And? Fuck dae ah dae now?'

'Like ah said, find oot where they're offte. Do ah have tae dae it masel?'

'That'd be magic Gal, wud ya? Wha good is this doin us anyway eh? Ahm fuckin freezin, pish wet an fuckin miles away from ma motor mind.' He paused. 'Ok got em at Haymarket.'

'What Haymarket? The station?'

'Aye the fuckin station, fair enough?'

'Where at Haymarket?'

'Bus stop.'

'Listen tae me, ya prick. Fuckin stay wi them. That's tae they actually gae somewhere, dunna gi a fuck how long that takes ok? Somewhere they might stay fur a wee whiley. Alright? Problem with that Dots an were gonna have words.' Galston hung up the phone.

Dots put the phone back in his pocket cursing and lit another cigarette. They were still at the bus stop, the fat one pacing, the other one just standing there, head down, hands in his jacket pocket. He stood and watched and waited.

He didn't have to wait long. He had just dropped the cigarette into a puddle when a car pulled up alongside the bus stop. He watched as words were spoken with the driver and then they moved to climb in.

He had a decision to make and made it without really thinking through the consequences. He sprinted across the street to the bus stop, knowing if they got into the car he had effectively lost them. He made the decision without really thinking what he would do once he got to them and within ten seconds found himself with this very dilemma. The fat one was already inside but the other one was standing at the rear door, presumably waiting for a child lock to be neutralised. He ran up and pushed James up against the door.

'Fuck you off tae pal?' These were the only words he managed to get out before finding himself being dragged backwards into the bus shelter. He struggled but couldn't find purchase with his feet or hands and ended up being dragged in a sitting position backwards into the recess of the bus shelter. He felt the water soaking through his jeans as he slid across the concrete slabs.

'Who the fuck are you?' an English voice shouted at him. Dots looked up at Tony.

Most people in this situation would be scared, very scared. Violence is not normally part of a normal person's experience. It's something that happens on TV, or to someone else. And as such, on the rare occasions they are presented with it, normal persons are normally frightened, terrified even. Dots on the other hand grew up with violence. His childhood was marked by it, and all his adult life it existed within the boundaries of his life. Violence for him was akin to commuting for a normal person, a bit of a pain, but nothing out of the ordinary. Being dragged backwards into a bus shelter, at night by a man significantly larger than himself didn't paralyze him with fear. On the contrary it was just part of the job and as such his reaction reflected this.

'Who the fuck are you?' he said, looking up from the cold concrete floor of the plastic shelter adding with a grin. 'Ya English cunt.'

Chapter 10

Bridgestone Manor is a large country house hotel sitting equidistant between Glasgow and Edinburgh. Built in the late 19th century as a summer retreat for one of the many industrialists who made their fortunes on the back of a burgeoning empire and its insatiable appetite for iron. Ships, bridges, factories, guns all required iron and the central belt of Scotland had more than its fair share of industrious men ready to take full advantage of this boom. They matched the readily available cheap labour coming off the boats from Ireland and down from the Highlands and the raw materials with the demand and built opulent houses and extravagant follies on the proceeds. The house was built in a Tudor style, open beams and large imposing fireplaces. It had twenty guestrooms, each tastefully decorated, a restaurant, and a number of private snugs. The American owners promoted it as a private getaway for business or pleasure and were happy to simply hand over the keys if the price was right. It was far enough away from any public road to be seen and in many cases heard. In short, for a fee, it was perfect for a group of people for whom privacy was paramount.

Upstairs in room eighteen Alexander (Sandy) Milne sat in a heavy leather chair. It had been a long time since he felt a stirring but as he watched the young girl writhe on the polished wooden floor in front of him he felt a movement and the faintest of tingling sensations in his groin. It was a sensation he had long given up on. She was young, probably twenty, he thought to himself as she pushed her blonde hair back and crawled on all fours towards him. The music was too loud for the house. The thump, thump of the bass vibrating all too easily through the old oak floorboards, at odds with the overall feel and ambiance of the place. The young girl didn't speak, she didn't need to and in any event her English was limited to all but a few basic words.

Sandy sat there and watched. Tight pale skin covered with a faint sheen of sweat, she glistened in the dull light. Kneeling before him she pulled his belt free. Sandy watched and tried to concentrate, the sensation was still there but he was still some way from where he needed to be. She handed him the belt and turned around with her hands behind her back. He did as was asked and tied her hands with his belt tight behind her back.

Amitra Smiritoff stared at the door as he tied her hands. She hoped he would respond. She knew who he was and had been told to please him. At sixteen Amitra was a three-year veteran in the job. She knew men and she knew pleasing men like Sandy was important.

Sandy watched her as she turned away from him lying down on her side before wiggling around and ending up face down, backside in the air directly in front of him. He stared at her invitation and tried to concentrate.

Downstairs Galston and a number of other men stood drinking as another two Amitras performed a well-choreographed act. They had done it so many times together it had become routine, they writhed around on the Persian rug together following the correct order of things as the group of men stood around them. The men didn't speak, they just watched in silence and of them only Galston felt uncomfortable with the situation. The phony act of lesbian passion did nothing for him. Added to this there were five men he knew very well standing close to him with visible erections. He wanted out of there. But he stayed; he played the game and waited. Eventually the girls reached the "climax" of their act and stood smiling before quickly leaving the room. Galston took the opportunity to leave as they were replaced by another young girl and a frightened-looking skinny black man. Good luck, he thought to himself as he walked towards the small bar in search of a drink.

Later that evening he and Sandy sat drinking whisky in front of an open fire in a snug. The party was still going strong in the room adjacent.

'Y'll no guess what the fuck happened today?' Sandy said, staring into the fire.

Galston looked over at him. 'What?'

'Got a call from Dennis Wessels.'

'Who?'

"Dennis Wessels, remember, the guy who gave us the Hinkinton job.'

'Aye right, what'd he want?' Galston perked up.

The Hinkinton job was a job Galston liked. Four years ago, it was an easy, scare and threaten type situation. A few choice words and the job was done. He had no idea how Sandy and Dennis had met and never thought to ask. It was corporate work, Hinkinton PLC was a global concern but geographically decentralised. In simple terms it was so dispersed the local team could do whatever they wanted, assuming it was within budget. Dennis Wessels, originally from the Netherlands was the general manager of the UK division. As it turned out, he would do whatever it took to deliver his numbers and for Galston it was very easy work that paid well.

'Has a thing for us.'

'A thing?'

'Right, a thing. He has it an wants a piece faer geeing it tae us.'

Galston and Sandy were about the same age and had known each other for over forty years. On nights like tonight Sandy would be his friend, his confidant. They would sip whisky and talk on the same level, world-weary man to world-weary man. Galston would act his part, going along with the charade but he knew the reality of the situation. They were not friends. Never had been. Galston did what Sandy told him to, he did it and got paid. It had been like that since the beginning. Galston just followed Sandy and as Sandy rose up, so did he. He knew him well and knew how to manage him. He also knew he would happily push him under a bus, both figuratively and physically in the blink of an eye. Sandy Milne was that sort of man. This was why he was so successful in his chosen line of work.

'Right.' Galston drained the heavy lead glass. 'Wha thing?

Sandy laughed. 'You'll no believe this.'

'Ok?'

'So, our cloggy friend Dennis left Hinkington a couple years ago, seems the top people decided tae start taking an interest in how they made their dough. Dennis didnae last long apparently.'

Galston smiled.

'You heard of Brown & Bingham?' Sandy asked looking at him directly.

Galston shook his head.

'Well anyway, he left Hinkington joined them, nae sure what he does there something tae dae with computer security.'

'Ok?' Galston wasn't entirely sure where this was going.

'Well it seems that Bingham has a problem, Dennis wants us tae help him oot.'

'Sort of problem?'

A young girl walked between them, naked, carrying a bottle of whisky. She made a point of bending over as she poured each of them a fresh dram.

Galston spoke after they both watched her leave. 'I canna dae this anymore, Sandy,' he said, indicating to the to the other room. 'Fine fer them but I canna barely ge' it up these days.'

'y'rather tea and scones Gal?' Sandy said directly without even a hint of humour.

Galston stared at his glass.

'Anyway, Dennis has a wee problem,' he continued.

Sandy then proceeded to walk Galston through all he knew at that point about Orchid. It could potentially be worth millions to their business, it seemed too perfect, almost a victimless crime and Sandy wanted a piece, a big piece, along with Dennis. Galston as usual would just do what he was told.

When he finished the monologue, Sandy smiled at Galston. 'Well?'

'What?'

'What dae you think?'

'Simple enough, Sandy, usual stuff, just maer money.'

Sandy nodded, he was getting excited. His abject failure with Amitra had disappeared from his mind. He had tried hard and Amitra for her part tried even harder but eventually they both conceded defeat. She left the room still naked with threats ringing in her ears. Sandy dressed himself and walked back downstairs fixing a grin on his face as he rejoined the other men.

Galston continued, 'Face o it, seems simple enough. How ya want me tae dae it, visit em? Who are they?'

Sandy leaned back on his chair, he sipped his dram and smiled broadly at Galston. 'Who are they?' he paused for effect before continuing. 'Dae you remember Maria, the tart who was fucked up?'

* * *

Galston and Sandy first met properly in January 1970. Prior to this he was aware of Sandy by reputation only. Most young men in the city were aware of Sandy Milne. His background was not very clear but by the time he was twenty-three years old in 1970 Sandy's name was linked tenuously with many crimes and murders across the city. At that point he had never been arrested and this only served to further fuel the myth and mystery surrounding him. The reality was Sandy had killed one man and this was only after the man in question had tried, unsuccessfully, to bury a broken glass in his throat. A minor verbal exchange in a pub was the spark and Sandy had tried to calm the man down as he wildly and drunkenly swung the jagged glass in his direction. Despite his warnings the man persisted and he ultimately ended up bleeding to death just around the corner from the bar. The police report detailed fifty stab wounds as the primary cause of death. It also surmised that the man had been restrained as the blows were delivered. Unsurprisingly no one in the bar recognised the two men who dragged the victim out of the bar that evening. Average clothing, average height, average everything. If Sandy's CV was light on the murder front it certainly wasn't in other criminal areas. For the past five years he had been running a very successful team of teenagers who sold drugs through three popular dancehalls and a plethora of stolen goods. Basically he sold whatever fell into his possession through a number of unlicensed markets throughout the city. From cigarettes to record players he sold it all.

He would use violence to protect his interests but only as a last resort, in a parallel universe he might have been seen as a businessman, an entrepreneur or even a leader. His team was made up of wayward teenagers aged between thirteen and eighteen. Recruitment wasn't difficult in the city and they were furiously loyal to him. His reputation and how he treated his "employees" was the key to this loyalty. He was a leader who preferred the carrot to the stick. This approach worked well with a group of young men who, in most cases, had never had a male role model worth looking up to in their short lives. To the rest of the city's underworld he was an up-and-comer who linked in well with the more traditional criminals in the city. He was astute enough to know his place and made sure the more powerful figures knew he knew this. His reputation soared and he rode this wave, fully understanding the power of an image. Perception is the truth and Sandy made sure the perception was exactly what he wanted it to be.

Sandy was also good friends with Brian Cox and six months after Tams death Galston was still prowling the city with vengeance on his mind.

Billy McNally's body had not been discovered for three weeks after Galston had bludgeoned him to death with the iron scaffold bar that late summer's evening. It was the smell that alerted the workmen to the decomposing body half buried in the sand behind the Portakabin. The subsequent police investigation found nothing and it was written off quickly. James, his brother, took Billy's death badly and was arrested five times in as many weeks for drunken disorderly behaviour. Like his brother, he had a tendency for booze and the death pushed him further down his own self-destructive path. Galston followed him regularly, just waiting for the right time, all the while continuing to fantasise about how he would do it. But after Billy, deep down, he knew it wouldn't be as the fantasy predicted.

The right time presented itself on a Saturday evening in late November. James was staggering around by himself. Slowly making his way in the general direction of home. Galston followed him some distance behind. He was slowly walking alongside the river, every so often steadying himself on the iron railing which followed he path. As he passed the South Portland Street Bridge he suddenly stopped, paused and then walked out onto the old iron footbridge. Galston watched him stagger to the middle and then lean over the edge. His could see his body retching and could hear a faint splash from his vomit splatting onto the surface of the river below.

This was his opportunity, James was presenting it to him, offering it to him. And Galston took it. He walked out onto the bridge. He continuously checked around for anyone else who might be watching. The middle of a bridge is an exposed position but it was deserted that evening. He walked fast to the centre of the bridge and without a word bent down, wrapped his arms around his thighs and stood up taking him with him. He then bodily threw him over the edge. James didn't make a sound or struggle and fell silently towards the dark water below. It was as if he was resigned to his fate, his body not even moving as he fell. The resulting splash broke the silence and Galston stood looking down as the water jumped and frothed and then quickly fell silent again. Its tar-like surface smoothed over. James disappeared. Galston stood there for ten minutes expecting to see him resurface and start swimming or at least to see the body floating but nothing. Nothing at all, it was if he had never existed. The river had taken him in one bite. He stood and smoked two cigarettes but nothing. The world was silent so he flicked the cigarette over the edge and turned for home. Again he felt nothing so his thoughts immediately turned to Brian Cox. He knew nothing about Brian. Never saw him in the usual places and had no real plan to speak of. He walked slowly, thinking. A sharp, cold breeze channelled its way up the river and with his collar turned up on his long thick coat he hunched over. He became just another dark shape in a night full of shadows moving slowly alongside the dark river.

* * *

Dots woke up with his face pressed into a coarse carpet. It was dark and he could feel the road beneath the car. He had figured out he was in the boot of a car but his memory was sketchy as to how he had ended up here. He could remember being dragged into the bus shelter and some big English fucker attacking him but he couldn't remember anything else. His head hurt like a bastard and the blood which flowed across his face was warm. Muffled voices filtered their way through to him.

'So what exactly are we going to do?' James asked, his voice surprisingly calm.

'We going to torture him, kill him?' Ewan asked from the passenger seat, his voice by contrast loaded with anxiety.

'Shut up would you, Ewan?' Tony said quietly from the driver's seat. 'No we are not going to torture him and kill him. Well we might. I don't know. What else was I supposed to do? He was there. Should I have left him?'

He continued, 'Look, I am still working this out, it was only a couple of hours ago I was happy drinking a beer totally unaware of all this shit. I figured he might come in useful – and anyway they fucking started it,' he said defensively. 'I will figure it out. Just at the moment we need to get the fuck away, ok?'

No one answered. The car fell silent again.

Tony hated not having a plan or a course of action to follow. He also knew that just reacting would most likely result in an outcome which they didn't want. He had to take the time to think it through. To do this he had to get as far away from danger as possible first and this was exactly what he was doing. He also mentally blocked out the other "at risk" people having realised shortly after leaving his house protecting all of them would simply be impossible. Certainly well beyond his capabilities. He hoped James and Ewan would agree with him. As he drove his mind was working over the options available to them. Whatever he did he would need to do it fast if he had any chance of protecting the girls.

They worked their way out of the city heading east and once they were on the city bypass they all relaxed a little. Traffic was light, three lanes empty but he drove carefully. Keeping the speed at just under 70mph. The conversation was muted. They mostly sat in silence.

It was Ewan who broke the silence sometime later. 'Where we going, Tony?'

'I have a house down here,' he responded nodding in the general direction of the windshield.

'Really? You have a house down here? Where?'

'Yes, Ewan, really I do. I have a house just south of North Berwick. A cottage.'

'Why?'

'What?'

'Why do you have a cottage in North Berwick?'

'Ewan, shut up would you please? I have a house down in North Berwick because I want to have a house in North Berwick, ok?'

'Sorry, was just asking. Seems strange to own a house in North Berwick, that's all.' He sounded slightly subdued.

'Ok then. Let's keep going. Why Ewan is it strange that someone would own a house in North Berwick. What's so fucking strange about North Berwick?'

'Have you ever been to North Berwick?'

'I own a fucking house there!'

James laughed.

'Of course I've been to North Berwick.'

'Guys calm down huh? Fine, you own a cottage in North Berwick Tony, sounds lovely. Ewan, Tony owns a house down here ok?' James was smiling as he spoke. It was the first time in a long time.

'Ok, just trying to make conversation. And Tony, why do I think it's strange for someone to own a house in North Berwick? It's strange because it's a fucking nothing place full of lost tourists looking for Berwick-upon-Tweed.'

'It's five miles south of North Berwick.'

'Ahhh, why didn't you say that in the first place. Now that makes perfect sense.'

They all laughed at this and the mood lightened in the car as they came to the end of the city bypass and headed along the A1.

Dots started kicking the back of the rear seat and shouting obscenities from the boot and the mood reverted back immediately.

* * *

January 1970. Galston had just finished a shift and was having a pint in the Flanders Bar just off Waterloo Street. He had left home the month before and was renting a small one-bedroomed place above a shop on Great Western road. Around about the time he left home he also started joining the groups of men going straight to the pub after their shift. He enjoyed the company more than the drink. It was a traditional Glasgow pub, thick mahogany bar, mirrors reflecting the optics, dim lighting and very few seats. The atmosphere was thick with smoke and heavy male conversation. He was standing talking to Jimmy Boyle a skinny man of about thirty years. Jimmy worked on the same shift as Galston but beyond that there was no other common denominator. They spoke about the upcoming old firm game as they drank their ale.

'Jimmy! Jimmy fuckin Boyle man,' a man walked between them both and grabbed Jimmy's hand. 'How you fuckin doing pal? Long time.'

'Aye Sandy it is, daein ok? Yerself?'

'Och you know Jimmy, scraping a living, you still oot at Goodyear?'

'Aye.'

'Fucksake man, ah told you tae come work faer me, I've got maer work than ah know what tae dae wit.' Sandy turned to look at Galston. 'Who are you?' he said directly at him.

Galston sipped his pint and stared back not answering, he didn't know who the man was but felt he probably wasn't going to like him.

'Galston. A mate of mine,' Jimmy said to break the standoff.

Sandy smiled at him. 'Galston, gud tae meet you, any pal of Jimmy's.' He glanced around the bar. 'Well you know, lemmi get you both a pint.'

'Nae worries, Sandy, we're fine,' Jimmy said, but Sandy ignored them and squeezed his way towards the bar.

Jimmy turned to Galston. 'Gal, listen dinnae fuck around with Sandy right, I know whit you're like but he could be fuckin trouble. Just drink his fuckin pint ok?'

Galston smiled at him. 'Dinnae worry Jimmy, I'll be fine.'

'You fuckin better be,' he said.

Sandy returned, a pint in each hand. 'Here you go boys,' he said, grinning.

'So, Galston, whit dae you do?' Sandy asked cheerfully.

Galston looked at him. Sandy was a few years older than him, blond hair with a friendly face. He was a thin man whose overall size hid an underlying strength, physical and mental. His smile was genuine though and despite his earlier misgivings he felt himself start to warm to him.

'Work with Jimmy,' he said nodding at his drinking companion.

'Goodyear?'

'Aye,' he sipped his pint again.

'Fuckin shithole there isn't it, you part the Union?'

'Ah have a choice?'

'Probably no, waste of time if you ask me, you pay em and they dae fuck all fur you.' Sandy was distracted by a sound coming from the other side of the bar. Raised voices which died down as quickly as they appeared.

'What is it you dae, Sandy?' Galston asked, he had already worked out who Sandy was but it seemed the appropriate thing to ask.

'I dae lots of things, Galston. Lots of things.' He was distracted again and then turned to Jimmy.

'Jimmy, remember Brian, Brian Cox?'

'Aye.'

'He's been down in London doing summing or other but is coming back next weekend. We're heading out for a few oan Saturday night if you fancy it?'

'I dunno, Sandy, need tae speak with the wife y'know?'

'For fuckssake, Jimmy, it's Brian, come oan, it'll be a fuckin laugh, bring yer pal here, the mare the merrier.'

'Will see ok?' Jimmy said non-committal.

'Aye ok Jimmy, 7 o clock here oan Saturday if you fancy it, anyway I'm off.' He shook Jimmy's hand and nodded at Galston.

Galston nodded in return and sipped his pint again, his mind was working furiously but his face remained calm.

'Dinnae know about you n your missus Jimmy but ah fancy a night oan the town,' he said.

* * *

Tony navigated the small steep country road, it was a single-track road but on an evening like tonight was deserted. He drove carefully with lights on full beam, the car bumped through deep puddled potholes and steam rose from the halogen lights. They wound their way down and pulled up outside a small, single-story, whitewashed cottage. It reminded James of the small fishing villages he would visit on the weekends in Fife as a kid.

'Ok, guys we're here.' He passed a set of keys to Ewan. 'You get inside and get the heating on. I'll deal with our friend.'

Ewan and James climbed out of the car. They could hear Dots shouting from the boot and could see the car rocking as he kicked and struggled within the confined space.

'You ever seen Goodfellas?' Ewan asked.

'Stop it, eh?' James said as he pushed open the door to the cottage. It felt cold and damp inside, he turned on the light and they both shuffled inside.

Tony stood looking at the boot of his car. He knew what was coming. The kicking and swearing from the boot told him this wasn't going to be easy. He had no real fear per-se but would much rather have a more compliant prisoner than a kicking and screaming one. His plan was to get him inside and secured. It was more a matter of how easy or difficult it would be and right then he wasn't in the mood for difficult. Sighing he took a deep breath and clicked the button on the boot. It popped open. Dots looked at him and his mouth formed into a bloody cartoon smile as he spoke. 'Hello, English cunt.'

The building, an old fisherman's cottage was small, squat and built to last. There were three rooms and a bathroom. The stone walls, a foot thick in places, were damp to touch. It had no central heating. Instead, in each room there was a small electric heater. The main room had an empty, soot covered, fireplace. James and Ewan walked through the cottage turning on heaters and lights. When finished they both stood waiting in the living room. The single, bare light bulb was bright and harsh. They stood squinting and not speaking. The charred smell of heaters not used for some time filled the damp space.

Dots tried to get out of the boot but the cramped conditions made the manoeuvre tricky. He had planned to jump out, cat-like, in a frenzy of kicking and punching. Instead he just moved viciously within the confines of the small space. He was swearing and sweating, frothy saliva formed in the corners of his mouth. Tony reached down and grabbed a fistful of his hair in an attempt to bring him under control but this just served to enrage him further. It felt like he was dealing with a wild animal as Dots bucked, kicked, spat and swore as he tried to get out. One of those poles with wire loops on the end for wild dogs would have been very useful, or a fucking taser, Tony thought before quickly realising it was never going to work. He changed tack and started punching him hard in the general direction of his head as he thrashed around. His fist connected with his face, his ear and the back of his skull. He kept doing it until the crazed animal eventually fell silent and still.

'Ewan, James – gimmi me a hand here would you?' he shouted breathlessly towards the cottage. His right fist was swollen and numb.

Thirty minutes later the three of them were sitting on the floor of the living room. There were no chairs. Ewan had found some old newspaper and wood and managed to get the fire lit. For the first time since they had arrived they started to feel warm. Dots was cable-tied unconscious to a chair in the bedroom.

'Nice place, Tony,' Ewan said from beside the fire. He had blood on his hands and steam was rising from his damp clothes. 'Anything to drink here?'

Tony ignored him, he sat with his back against the far wall staring at the fire.

'What are we going to do, Tony?' It was James.

Tony shook his head. 'We need to speak with him,' he said, indicating to the door. 'We need to find out what's going on firstly. Secondly what they know and then I can figure out what we can do.'

Ewan stood up. 'Let's go ask him then.'

'Why you so keen all of a sudden Ewan?' James asked.

'What?'

'Why are you suddenly so fucking keen to start doing people over eh?' James's tone was direct and accusatory.

'I dunno, James, I want to get this over as much as you do. Am fuckin shiteing maself the same as you.'

'Right, sure, Ewan.'

'Listen both of you, let's get this sorted and we can get back to whatever we want to ok?' Tony said, trying to diffuse the situation.

'Craig's fucking dead, Tony, no one's going back to anything.' James's voice was raised, he remained staring at Ewan. 'Craig's dead and I want to know why.'

'We know why,' Ewan said calmly.

'No we fuckin don't Ewan. We know he's dead yes. We don't know why, well I certainly don't. Why him? Why not you? Why not me?' He paused. 'Why in fucking Switzerland? How the fuck did they know we would be there anyway. How did they know this? Been thinking about that. Only you, me and Craig knew where we were going. I know I certainly didn't tell them. I am pretty fucking sure Craig didnae so I'm wondering who did.'

'You think I did?' Ewan's voice was also raised and he started walking towards James.

'Pack it in the pair of you will you. For fuckssake, now is not the time for this. We need to hold ourselves together.' Tony walked between them.

'You think I did it do you?' Ewan ignored Tony. 'Go on, James, is that what you think? You think I fuckin killed him, ya prick?'

Before James could answer a mobile phone started ringing, it was distant but clear.

'Whose is that?' Tony said.

'Dunno, not mine,' Ewan said.

'Mine neither,' James said, still looking at Ewan.

Tony threw open the door to the bedroom and the ringtone got louder. He felt Dot's pockets and found the phone, it was still ringing as he pulled it out then stopped. He looked at the display, it told him he had missed one call from "Gal". He took it back to the living room quietly cursing himself for not checking his pockets. Basic stuff, Tony. The interruption had broken the standoff between Ewan and James. They watched Tony, not talking.

* * *

Galston stretched out on the leather couch and put the phone down. It had been two hours since Dots had phoned him and he was starting to wonder. He had been dozing on the couch, for some reason he thought it would be wrong to sleep in the bed. He had killed the guy's friend, had punched him, broken into his house and terrorised him sufficiently to have him wandering around the city piss wet through. But somehow sleeping in his bed seemed wrong. It crossed an imaginary moral line in Galston's head if there ever was such a thing. He lay there and stared at the ceiling. He could hear the rain outside and the occasional car work its way past the flat. Where the fuck was Dots?

* * *

Tony held out the phone as he walked in. 'Looks like they are starting to worry.'

James looked over. 'Is he awake?'

Tony shook his head and stood studying the phone. He flicked through the recent calls, all to the same person "Gal". Ewan and James watched him as he paced back and forth.

'Fuck it,' he said decisively and went back to the bedroom. He returned dragging Dots with him and placed him in the centre of the room with his back to the fire and then immediately started slapping his face. Blood from the various open wounds on his face spattered on the floor and the wall as his head rocked side to side. Tony kept slapping him, the sound echoing in the small room. James and Ewan watched. The slapping continued until eventually Dots opened his eyes, loosely and unfocused at first then quickly sharpening. Through the bloody swollen face he looked around with a steely determination. When he spoke, it was with a frothy drunk man speech. His jaw, broken from the first encounter at Haymarket, moved strangely out of sync with his lips.

'Scho what the now, Englissh cunt?' he looked at Tony. 'Gonna fuhcking kill mhe?'

Tony didn't speak. He took a photograph of Dots on the phone and sent it to the person called Gal, who he assumed was part of this. He watched the phone as the message sent.

Eventually he spoke. 'Let's see shall we?'

Twenty minutes later Ewan and James were sitting on the floor leaning against the internal wall. They sat and watched quietly. Dots was sitting cable-tied tight to the wooden dining chair in the middle of the room, he had stopped struggling now. His head hung limp and blood ran down his face, pooling on his chin and then dripping onto his lap. To Ewan and James he looked a broken man, his face swollen and bloody but neither of them could be certain. They had just seen him take a serious pounding and still come back for more. They had also both seen the video of Craig.

Tony also didn't know how far to take it. He needed information, something to give him, give them, an advantage. At present they had nothing. For the time being they were out of harm's way but there were other people beyond the cottage who were also at risk. He needed information quickly and had to get it, one way or another. He had trained in interrogation but had never actually done it, for real. He knew the basics so knew that absolute violence or threats of violence just didn't work. It could, in some instances prove fatal, or just elicit lies. People would say anything to stop the pain. Either way there was no guarantee of him getting what he needed. He needed to know where to find this person called Gal and from there he would work his way up the tree assuming Gal wasn't the top. This was the extent of his plan at present.

He found what he was looking for in the kitchen and moved back to the living room.

Dots appeared unconscious or asleep to Tony but he was alive. He could see him breathing and this was good enough. He looked at Ewan and James and then turned back to his prisoner. Laying the kitchen knife on the floor he pulled his head up. Dots grinned drunkenly at him and then the phone rang, it was loud and everyone, including Dots, jumped at the sound.

The caller ID read "Gal".

'Hello,' Tony said into the phone staring at Dots. He was watching him back.

'Who's this?' Galston asked.

'Right, let's start the opposite way round shall we? Who are you?' Tony replied flatly.

Galston laughed, he stood up and walked to the window of James's flat, the street was silent outside. It was just after midnight.

'Ok, look we could dance aroond fer a while but a havnae got the energy. Ahm knackered. Ya need tae tell those two fuckers tae do wha we say. Ahm getting a little bored wi this. Have ya seen the video ah sent? Hope so, might gi ya something tae think aboot whilst you are making up yer mind.'

Tony shook his head. 'No I haven't but I heard about it. You've probably seen the photograph I sent you as well, don't think for a second we will not reciprocate in kind. I am a very different animal from these two. You really need to start understanding this fast,' he said indicating to James and Ewan.

'These two? Ok, so am nae the smartest man in the world but that means you only have the two of em wit you, which means ahm guessing mind, the girls are nae with you. So ah'll say this one maer time just in case you havnae been listening or you're just basically ah stupid cunt. Tell em tae dae exactly what ah say or ah'll start lopping feet off of the kids. Dinnae make the mistake of thinking ah willnae. You might no believe it but ah dislike this as much as you dae, but ah will fuckin dae it.'

He paused to let this sink in.

'Naw we can gae on, threatening each other whit whatever the fuck we like but here's what ah suggest. You dae whit the fuck you like tae Dots. Boil him alive in oil for aw ah care an then you let the other two know ahm on ma way tae start mutilating their women and kids ok? Ahm gonna hang up now, please believe that ah'll dae whit ah say so ah suggest you act oan it.'

Tony didn't answer.

Galston hung up the phone and sighed still staring out over the wet street. He hated messing with kids.

Chapter 11

Restaurant Widder is situated at an altitude of 1800m. Halfway up the mountain and excluding the multitude of small cafes and snow bars it's the highest proper restaurant in the valley. In wintertime it's only accessible by sled or on foot either up from the valley or using the cable car and walking down a short torch-lit path. In the summer time, once the road is open, it becomes a fixed lunch stop for the many bus tours that toured the country. Sabine held Craig's hand as they walked up the steps to the restaurants main entrance. They had travelled to the base of the path by horse drawn sled. It took them from a designated pick up point in town to the restaurant by way of a scenic route. They were pulled up along a snow-covered avenue of trees, the only sound being the swish of the sled and the odd clink of the horses bridle. As they sat in the carriage, they held hands under the thick blanket covering them and watched, mesmerised by the view as they worked their way up the mountain side. Steam rose from the horse which pulled them and the driver kept his eyes firmly ahead allowing the couple privacy to enjoy the, as adver-tised, romantic evening. They kissed at some point along the way. It was an intimate kiss.

There were two buildings; a main house and further down in the garden was a small den. The den was just large enough for a small table and as they passed it candle lights flickered through the frosted windows. Sabine had booked the den, a private dinner for two persons. It was part of the overall romantic evening package. They entered the large house and waited for someone to notice them standing there. It was very warm and the sounds of hushed conversations and cutlery flowed out of the main dining area. The warmth, the sounds mixed with the smell of heavy alpine food and wood smoke was intoxicating. They stood holding hands, not speaking, Craig didn't want the evening to end before it had even begun. Sabine didn't want it to begin and she gripped his hand tightly.

* * *

Gustl Ernhoffer became a father figure to Sabine. With a shaven head, heavy muscular build and dark skin he cut an imposing figure. The only indication he was fifty years old were the lines on his dark suntanned face. Gustl could move around the gymnasium with the speed and grace of a man half his age. Sabine and her fellow students would sit cross-legged on the polished wooden gymnasium floor and watch him demonstrate the moves and then try to repeat them. He would walk around, barefooted and speak to them all calmly and firmly. He was in charge, of this there was no doubt.

A month earlier Sabine had stood on the rusting fire escape of the Spital Heidelberg smoking what would be her last cigarette. The bruises on her face were raw and swollen but it was the indescribable internal pain which bothered her the most. Deep inside she throbbed and constantly ached. The female doctors were sympathetic to an extent but she could sense an under-current. She sensed what they were thinking even if they wouldn't admit it to themselves. She's a prostitute, what did she think would happen? Stupid bitch, probably deserved it. Sabine saw this and avoided eye contact with them. She knew what they were thinking, but needed them so she had to stay and endure it. She wanted to run out of the place, run back to her small apartment and hide. She could barely walk so she stayed and let them do their work.

That morning a male doctor had explained the extent of her injuries. None of them were life-threatening he told her, however, there would be pain and bleeding for some time to come. She had asked him if she was pregnant, he shook his head 'I don't think so, but best to test in a week or so'. He handed her a morning-after pill, 'Take this as well, just to be sure.'

The warm rain fell on her and soaked through the thin hospital gown, it felt delicious as she drew deeply on the cigarette. She could feel the industrial-sized sanitary pads stretching out her underwear, one at the front, one at the back. She stared out over the grey industrial park next to the hospital and started planning what she would do.

She had glimpsed the newspaper the previous day and knew her situation had been covered. They had named her and why she was on the base in the first place, so it was only a matter of time before she was asked to leave the university. She would try to argue her case, but in matters such as this, embarrassing matters, the result were normally clear cut.

Never again would she find herself in such a situation.

Never again would she be so hopelessly incapable of defending herself or doing anything about it. The memories were fresh, raw. Burned into her brain. Forced down, the smell of beer and cigarettes, laughing, music, deep voices. She had tried to joke her way out of it but screamed as the older one roughly pushed her down to the floor, he held her face squashed hard against the stone floor. She screamed so they gagged her and continued.

She lost count how many, it became a blur, sometimes they would be gentle, sometimes not. Sometimes they used objects, bottles, a brush handle and more than once there was more than one. She passed out at one point certain she was going to die.

Standing on the old rusting fire escape that wet afternoon she made a vow to herself, to change, to take charge. And she did. She threw herself into a regime of martial arts and basic common-sense training. It would never erase the memories but with time she didn't want them to be erased, it had happened, it was part of her. The world to that point for her had been a happy, shiny thing to be experienced and enjoyed. Now it was a dark and dangerous place and she was going to be ready for it. It took her two years until she felt properly whole again, ready to face the world.

They kicked her out of university soon after she returned. It came as no surprise and was actually a relief. She was quickly ostracised by her friends, no one would speak to her. Her carefree student existence had disappeared overnight. Sabine left Heidelberg quietly and moved to Munich. Home wasn't an option either. She found a job working the till in a supermarket.

It was in Munich she met Gustl.

She was a good pupil. She enjoyed the physicality of the sport. She enjoyed the practical elements of learning how to defend herself and took pleasure in learning how to hurt someone physically. It surprised her how much she enjoyed this and the confidence it gave her was a revelation. She too could physically hurt someone, it was possible, she could act, do something and hurt another human being. The first time she had to punch someone was difficult. Punching a leather bag was, she discovered, a very different proposition to punching a real person and it didn't come easy to a woman who had never done such a thing in her life.

She did it tamely and Gustl laughed, he pushed her and she fell to the floor. He held out his hand and she stood back up.

'Now punch me,' he said again.

She did a little harder and again she found herself on the floor, she was starting to get annoyed both at Gustl's strength and her pathetic response.

'Will you punch me properly please? Do it for real. Do it hard. I won't break and you need to know how it feels.' He spoke to her calmly, Gustl, someone she could trust. He kept repeating this until eventually she was punching as hard as she could, she was laughing as she threw the punches.

'Ok. Good,' he said breathlessly. 'Let's put you up against someone now.'

And so it went on, her training, her education. She learned, grew fitter and walked taller. The night she limped off the American base her life changed and the world around her changed. Gustl lifted her up and she emerged a different person, a changed woman. A better and stronger woman.

She started meeting men for money again not long after arriving in Munich. It was less of a nice supplemental income at that point, it had become a real economic need.

Her internal warning system was still intact. She became even more careful, never would she walk into the unknown again.

One September evening she was escorting a man back to his hotel room. They had enjoyed a drink in a local bar, chatted, drank a little and sorted out the money. He was in his mid-thirties, unhappily married he told her. Sabine listened and smiled her work smile. They were walking back arm in arm when he suddenly dragged her down an alley.

'Let's fuck here now,' he said, pressing her hard against the cold bricks, his hands running up the insides of her thighs. His mouth pressing against hers, tongue trying to force open her lips.

Four minutes later Sabine had a choice to make. He was lying on the ground not moving much, still alive but heavily concussed. She stood over him for a minute and then walked away.

* * *

Galston took the cable car in the darkness to the restaurant. He had a large rucksack on his back and felt conspicuous amongst the other well dressed diners filling the space. It was dark outside and the car lurched as it cleared a pylon and continued its upwards momentum. His stomach flipped as it did so, fear wasn't something which he had much experience of but he felt distinctly uneasy inside this metal box suspended high above the valley. It quietly rushed through the night. He could faintly see some lights outside through the frosted Plexiglas but had no concept of where he was in relation to them. Sometimes the car would judder and slow down or drop down or speed up. His ears popped and he held on tightly to the railing, focusing his attention on the other occupants of the cable car. They appeared relaxed and he tried hard to do the same.

* * *

The waiter took Sabine and Craig's jackets, their drinks order and disappeared. They were alone in the small wooden cabin situated just below the restaurant.

Looking around Craig spoke, 'Where's the toilet?'

Sabine smiled and indicated back towards the main building, 'Up there I think or,' she looked outside, 'out there?'

'I'll wait.'

Candles provided the only light in the cabin and an open fire crackled to one side, similar to the main house it was very warm and they sat across from each other. Craig held out his hand and she took it.

'Craig, I've got something to tell you,' she said, her face dark and unsmiling. She had been thinking about it all day and had decided to tell him, to warn him. She realised earlier that the feelings for him were real. She knew he was in trouble but had no concept why and what the implications were. Her assumption on how bad they were had been multiplying in her head. She had also been wracking her brains as to how to not be part of it, or at least in his mind. The man wouldn't kill him, he would survive and afterwards she would be there. This was plan A but as the day progressed she moved to plan B, tell him the truth. Well at least some of the truth.

Craig shook his head. 'Don't. Dinnae go spoiling this please. Tell me tomorrow at the airport. Tell me afterwards.'

She sat looking at him thinking.

'Craig, it's important, I think…well, I have…I need to tell you something.'

He looked at her and squeezed her hand.

'Ok, can I have a drink and something to eat first? Don't want you to go spoiling the food and wine before I've had any.' He smiled as he spoke.

'Ok.' She smiled a thin smile in return.

The waiter returned with a bottle of red wine and a basket of bread. They sat silently as he poured a sample for Craig to taste, he swirled it, sipped it and nodded his approval. The waiter poured two generous glasses and disappeared again into the frozen night.

* * *

The cable car moved slowly into position and the doors groaned as they opened. The driver indicated with his arm the direction of the restaurant and the diners nodded at him as they left. Galston was the last to leave, he nodded at the man as well. It was freezing and he followed someway behind the other diners down a steep foot-path lit up with torches. He could see the path snaking its way down and ending abruptly at the bright lights of the restaurant. It looked like the path was on fire from his elevated perspective and Galston liked it.

* * *

'Why?' Craig asked Sabine.

She had just finished talking in glowing terms about her love for martial arts.

'Why what?'

'Why kung fu? Why not yoga? Or Badminton?'

She thought about it for a while before answering.

'Because I want to be tough,' she was smiling as she spoke but Craig sensed there was some truth in her answer.

'Okay,' Craig said dubiously. 'Are you tough?'

'Wanna test me?'

'No, not really, I really don't fancy being beaten up by a girl.'
He paused. 'I much prefer what we were doing earlier, but it
does explain how come you are so bendy.'

Her face lit up. 'Yes, I am aren't I?'

Craig sat back and sipped his wine. He was falling deeper and
deeper for this girl and a rush of conflicting thoughts clouded his
mind.

The waiter returned again, he entered the cabin quietly and
quickly served the starters, two tiny winter salads. The fire
crackled and spat hot embers against the fire-guard.

* * *

Galston reached the restaurant and stood thinking, where? He
walked around and saw the cabin set away from the main
building. It was small and he could see the shimmer of light
through the small windows. Further down below, the mountain
slipped away towards the town. He could see the street lights in
the distance. To the left were steep cliffs, and to the right, was
what looked like a road lined with trees. He walked towards the
trees following the path which was no longer lit. It was freezing
and his breath steamed as he walked. He pulled up the hood on
his jacket and lit a cigarette. His gloves made smoking difficult
but he persevered.

* * *

By the time the main course arrived the bottle of wine had been
consumed. Both Craig and Sabine faces were flushed with the
heady mixture of heat and alcohol.

'So what were you going to tell me earlier?' Craig asked
Sabine as he cut into his pork steak.

She chewed her mouthful and looked away. Suddenly everything was possible. They could have a future, why not? The wine

and the evening had changed her mind again and she turned back to him with a smile.

'It can wait, enjoy your food.'

The waiter brought the second bottle of wine and poured them both a glass, he smiled at them and Craig thanked him. As soon as he left, Craig stood up and walked around the table, he kissed her.

'I have wanted to do that all evening,' he said half kneeling on the floor.

'And I wanted you to do that all evening, really.'

'Let's leave soon. I want to feel you naked,' Craig whispered in her ear.

She looked away towards the fire.

* * *

Galston dumped the rucksack at the side of the road, next to a signpost and looked back up the hill. The restaurant was in sight. He couldn't see the town but he knew it would be visible just around the next corner. The road was snow-covered, trees lined the route all the way to town. Galston tried to imagine it in summer time, the snow gone, green and pine trees all around. Cars rushing by. The tree-lined route would be popular with tourists and outdoor types but a few steps away from the road, into the trees would be a land almost untouched by man. It was perfect, so he left the rucksack next to the post, and started back up the hill.

* * *

Sabine glanced at her watch and looked around the cabin. Craig had gone to the toilet. It was as romantic a setting as she had seen. The fireplace, the dinner and the company. She stared at the fireplace and wondered when it would all come crashing down.

She didn't want it to end.
She loved him.

* * *

Galston stood just below the cabin and smoked a cigarette. He was warm from walking back up the hill and stood looking down on the town far below. Wood smoke from the cabin filled the air around him. He smoked and waited.

* * *

At the urinal in the main house Craig stood and wobbled a little. The fresh air from the short walk had spun his head slightly and he smiled to himself. What was it she wanted to tell him? He was intrigued but didn't want to know at the same time. He knew it would probably spoil the evening whatever it was. Real life was starting to close in on them and he wanted to delay the inevitable. It would still be there tomorrow whatever it was. He zipped himself up and turned to wash his hands. The water was warm and he studied his face in the mirror as the tap gurgled away. What was he doing? He knew deep down what he had to do, he had already made his mind up. He couldn't live with himself if he didn't do it before they left each other in the morning. His stomach was tight as the thoughts started to burst open in his head. Tell her now he said to himself in the mirror.

* * *

Galston dropped the remnants of his cigarette and stomped it into the snow at his feet. He wasn't worried about leaving evidence, DNA or the like. He had never really bothered himself with such things in the past and so far this approach had served him well. Normally, though, the people he killed were people for whom he suspected the police would take one look and determine they had it coming. Low-level gangster wannabes, drug dealers, pimps. He was doing them a favour, one less wanker criminal wandering the streets for them to worry about. No, they would fill out the forms, tick the boxes or whatever it was they did and then move on, filing them away in the low priority cabinet below the missing cat section. Missing kids, paedophiles, rapists were prioritised far above any crime he committed and he liked it this way. Best all round for everyone. He stretched his feet inside his boots, they were very cold and his beard felt stiff when he touched it. It was frozen and he cursed this job. Get it done and get the fuck out of this frozen country. He turned and saw Craig returning to the cabin. He waited until he was inside and then headed up the steps towards the door.

* * *

As Galston headed out that Saturday night in January 1970 he was in a murderous rage. He had worked himself up and into it. All day images of Brian laughing as he walked away from Tam's lifeless body filled his mind. It was the mindlessness of it which really wound him up. They did it because they could, because they felt like it. Because it was a laugh. No other good reason. Galston and Tam were minding their own business that evening, talking, laughing and kicking a ball, nothing more. They were bored, drunk and fancied a bit of fun, it could have been anyone at all. But it wasn't anyone at all so Galston had worked himself up and the darkness had descended. He got himself ready, fresh clean trousers and shirt and imagined walking into the bar wielding the WWII bayonet he had recently acquired. He would walk in, straight up to Brian and without saying a word stab him in the throat. He would stab him hard. So fucking hard that the handle would be pressed against the skin, his fist just under his chin with the end of the blade protruding a few inches out of the back of his neck. He fantasised about watching the life drain out of him as he stood there, blood flowing over the handle and his fist. He imagined the bar falling silent as he did it then pulling the bayonet back and Brian crumpling to the floor. He imagined all of this as he combed his dark hair in front of the small cracked mirror. The fantasy satisfied the urges inside him and he smiled as he saw Brian's lifeless body lying in a puddle of fresh warm blood on the wooden floor boards of Flanders bar. He pulled on his long winter jacket, fed the bayonet into the deep inside pocket and left his flat.

Outside was dark and wet, grey people walked quickly. It wasn't an evening for hanging around. Leaving his close, he turned right and marched purposefully down Great Western road. He would walk this way every morning to start his shift, hundreds of other men just like him would walk the route. Tonight though he was almost alone and this suited him. He walked quickly and within ten minutes was pushing open the stained glass door to the bar. It was 7.30pm, January 25th 1970 and the direction of Galston's life was about to abruptly change direction. He had just turned eighteen.

He pushed open the door, the heat and smell of the bar contrasted starkly with the dreich weather outside. He felt dizzy. The smell was the sour beer smell from his childhood. Smoke filled the room and conversations were deep, working-class male conversations. He had one hand on the bayonet as he scanned the room. He saw them in the corner, eight of them standing in a circle, each holding a pint, Brian was talking and everyone was laughing. Brian, good-looking, happy and the centre of attention. He saw Sandy but not Jimmy, the other men he knew by sight but no more. Galston didn't hesitate, he started edging his way through the crowd towards them, his hand felt clammy on the hard steel handle but he kept going. The rage he felt in seeing Brian's smiling face overwhelmed him. It took over his total being. He wasn't in charge of his body at that moment, the darkness was absolute and as he approached the men he started pulling the weapon from his jacket.

Sandy saw him approaching and immediately walked towards him, they met in the middle of the room, shoulder to shoulder with other drinkers. He put an arm around his shoulder and turned him towards the bar.

'Nae here,' he said firmly into his ear. 'Nae here. Nae now.'

Galston was shocked, stunned and felt his momentum slipping, he was close enough to Brian, three more steps and he would be directly in front of him. He started to shrug Sandy's arm off and Sandy gripped him more firmly.

'Are you a fuckin eejit? Ah said, nae now, nae here. Later.'

'What t fuck are you gaen on aboot?' Galston asked releasing his hand from the bayonet and turning to face Sandy. 'What t fuck dae you think am gaen tae dae?' He spoke without fear or anger. His voice was direct and calm.

Sandy smiled and walked him towards the bar and spoke in a hushed tone. 'You ken who ah am Galston din ya?'

Galston nodded.

'Then ya'll also know, ahm good, very fuckin good at whit ah dae. Ah know a lot of stuff and ah also know you are aboot tae fuck over Brian over there,' he nodded his head in their direction. 'Ah ken why, ah also know that it wis you who did in the McNallys.'

Galston was stunned.

'Aye, ah fuckin know a lot ok, just accept it. Ah also know if you kill Brian in here, right now, it'll be the last fuckin thing you dae.'

'You think?'

'No, ya stupid cunt, I know it. You dae that 'n aboot a second later ah'll shoot you in the fuckin head.' He partially opened his jacket and Galston saw the handle of a pistol pushed into the waist of his trousers.

'Ah'll shoot you in the head because that's whit's expected, I won't want tae dae it, but ah will dae it, you better fuckin believe me. Now, you stand here. Ah'll buy you a pint, which you will drink. Ah'll then introduce you tae that bunch a wankers over there and we will have a nice evening ok?'

Galston didn't speak, he was still stunned by the turn of events.

'You will fuckin enjoy the evening and then later, when ah say so, you can have Brian.'

'When ah fuckin say so,' he repeated.

Sandy then turned to the barman and ordered Galston a pint of ale. Galston stood there, his heart beating hard, his face covered with a sheen of sweat. A pint appeared in front of him and as he lifted it his hand shook so violently he spilled some of it onto the mahogany bar.

'Calm a fuck down, Galston eh?' Sandy said to him leaning forward. 'Drink yer pint and then come over, say hi tae me and ah'll dae the rest, ok.'

Galston picked up the pint with both hands and sipped the dark brown liquid.

'Ok?' Sandy asked again.

He just nodded and took a deeper drink from his glass.

Sandy left him there and returned to the crowd. Galston heard him saying something about a younger brother of someone or other. He took big gulps from his pint and stared at his reflection in the mirror behind the bar. He was seconds away from murdering Brian, seconds, and now with the dregs of a pint in his hand he felt so far away from the act it shocked him. Sandy changed it all and as the adrenaline left his body he felt dazed. He finished the pint and indicated to the barman for another. The darkness had left him for now, he was just Galston McGee again. He took one sip from the pint and then turned towards the group of men in the corner smiling. Sandy studied him carefully as he approached then smiled broadly as he introduced him to the group of men. Galston nodded in their direction as he said their names.

'So where you working the now, Gal?' Sandy said and the conversations started up again, Galston was just another member of the group. He talked, nodded, laughed and drank, his subterfuge always at the back of his mind but it came easier to contain as the night progressed. As the pints disappeared he relaxed more and more.

Four hours later they were sitting in the Market Bar, a tiny bar located in a basement on Renfrew Street. Most of the group had dispersed, off in search of women or heading home to the wife. The bar was empty but so small that Sandy, Galston, Brian and Donny Mackenzie, another friend of Sandy's, virtually filled it. The barman was an old silver-haired man, white hair, white beard – a skinny Santa Claus Brian had called him as they entered.

'So who dae ya hang aroond wi Galston?' Brian asked. 'Havnae seen you around much.'

Sandy answered him. 'No like you've been around fer a while Bri, surprised you member anyone.' He paused to sip his pint. 'Wha the fuck were yah dain doon in London anyhow? Ah hear ya can make good money doon there as a rent boy, pretty man like n all.' He leaned both elbows on the table as he spoke.

'Fuck off, Sandy, huh, was dain this and that.' Brian turned towards the barman. 'Hoi Santa, gonna gaet us a round of wee ones eh?'

The barman looked back at him for longer than was polite and then turned to the optics.

'You shud get a scar or two, toughen up that face o yaers Bri,' Sandy continued. 'Too pretty, faer too fuckin pretty. How much you charge fer a blow job?' His voice had lost the humour and Galston picked up on an almost imperceptible atmospheric change.

'Sandy, fuck off eh. Ah made good money down there and didnae have to suck a single cock right?'

Sandy stood up. 'Aye, right Brian whitever ya say, where's the pisser in here?' he said looking at the barman, who nodded to a small battered door to the left of the bar.

Brian continued as Sandy left the bar. 'Aye good money, easy dough n all, streets r paved wit fuckin gold doon there yah ken?'

'How much ya make, Brian?' Donny asked. Galston sat quietly, not speaking just listening and watching the toilet door.

Brian took out his wallet and opened it up for both of them to see, it was packed with £10 notes. 'Plenty,' he said grinning. 'Weeuns are oan me.'

Sandy came out of the toilet, the door swung behind him and he just stood there surveying the bar, the barman watched him, Galston watched him, he stood there and looked different. The smile had gone and his eyes were focused. Brian was shoving the heavy wallet back in his pocket with his back to the toilet. Sandy looked at the barman and then took three paces and grabbed Brian's hair without speaking. He dragged him backwards towards the toilet door. Brian, surprised, struggled and gasped at the pain, he fell backwards to the floor and Sandy quickly dropped down and kneeled on his shoulders.

'The fuck you daen, Sandy? You gaen fuckin mad?' Brian was struggling to sit up but not too forcefully. After all this could still be a game.

'Havnae gaen mad, Brian, like ah said, you caed dae with a scar or two. Burds'll love it.' He was leaning over him, his blond hair hanging down.

Donny and Galston sat quietly. Donny was agitated, Galston was calm.

'Come oan now, take this outside huh? Nae in here,' the barman said, rooted to the spot behind the tiny wooden bar.

Sandy looked at him. 'Ya know, friend, if ah wis you ah'd shut the fuck up. Go lock the door and dinnae worry. Dinnae be a prick an ah'll saert you out. Fuck aboot an its gunna git messy ok?'

The barman looked at him not sure what to do.

'Gae lock the fuckin door!' he repeated, and then, 'Gal, dae it would you?' he said without looking up.

Brian started to struggle more forcefully. He was bucking up trying to knee Sandy in the back as he twisted his torso. 'Gaet the fuck off me Sandy wud ya, pack it in eh,' he gasped.

Sandy ignored him and turned to Galston, 'Gimmi that blade of yours Gal wud ya?'

Galston removed the bayonet from his jacket and walked over to them. He held the blade out and smiled at Brian. 'You know, Brian, ya daft cunt – ya really should have minded me,' he said before walking over and locking the door, there was a small curtain which he drew closed. As he did so he could see shadows of people walking by above, the orange streetlight stretching and bending them into grotesque shapes.

He turned back to the room and watched Sandy press the tip of the bayonet into Brian's cheek, he was holding it like a pen, carefully. Brian was squinting to see it. 'Naw dinnae move, Bri, might slip and dae some serious damage. Take yer eye oot or summing.'

The barman stood still behind the bar unsure what to do.

Donny sat quietly watching them, he was equally unsure how to act, he wanted to run but couldn't.

Sandy smiled at Brian and then pushed the blade into his cheek. The tip pierced the skin and blood ran down the side of his face, he then dragged the handle down creating a wound running from below his eye to his chin. Brian was quiet as he cut him, he winced and squirmed but didn't scream or shout.

'There you gae Bri, much better, maer manly. Hey, Santa, whatcha think?' Sandy said, cheerfully surveying his work before standing up and walking back to the table leaving him lying on the floor.

The atmosphere changed again. The barman moved and Donny shifted in his seat. Brian stood up, his hand pressed against his cheek, blood was flowing through his fingers and down his arm but he didn't react violently, he didn't react at all – he just stood where he was. He knew Sandy well and regardless of the pain or humiliation he knew better.

As Sandy sat down he passed the bayonet back to Galston, he sipped his pint and then spoke, 'Dae whit you like naw, ' he said to him.

Galston immediately stood up, firmly gripped the handle and walked quickly over to Brian. 'Wha the fuck dae you—' was all Brian managed to get out before Galston thrust the bayonet deep into his neck. He stopped speaking the moment the long blade tore through his larynx. It ripped an inch-wide hole in his neck and exited through his spine, crushing bone and severing nerves. Brian's hands instinctively moved to the blade but the connection between hand and brain had already been lost. He stood there holding Galston's hand but not really knowing it. His eyes were wide open in fear as blood sprayed out, covering them both. Galston stood still, firmly holding the bayonet and watched the life quickly drain out of his eyes. He watched them stare at him and then turn glazed and unfocused. With his other hand he stopped Brian from falling. He held him upright and watched him die. 'Tam Hellman you fucker, that's why,' he said, as the final signs of life and accusation left Brian's body. He then pushed him backwards and let his body fall with the handle still buried in his neck. Brian's head hit the edge of the bar with a sickening crack and then flopped on the floor. He ended up, half in the serving area, half out. His body convulsed and twitched as a pool of blood spread out over the floor.

Galston stood still breathing deeply, his shirt shining slick wet with blood, his heart was pounding, he watched Brian's body twitch one last time then stop forever. He felt excitement, elation, unlike the McNally brothers he really felt this. His whole being was tingling. He was enjoying it.

Sandy was sitting at the table watching him. He drained his

pint before speaking.

'Think it's Brian's round right?' And then, looking at the barman, 'Ya gonna serve us those shorts anytime soon, Santa?'

* * *

Craig walked back into the cabin. Sabine was sitting staring at the fire. The room was very warm and smelled of food and wood smoke. He walked over to her and put his hand on the back of her head.

'I think I have fallen for you, I really want to tell you this,' he said quietly. His heart was pounding and his voice shaking. He was nervous, even with the wine. This woman excited him in a way he never thought possible, she was beautiful, sexy, funny. He was terrified she would leave, back to whatever her life was in Germany. Leave him with an ache of what might have been, the possibilities were endless and he could see this now. It would be messy, very messy but he wanted it regardless of the pain to come. He wanted her to know it even if she told him she was married or whatever it was she had wanted to tell him earlier. He had to tell her because the alternative of keeping quiet was too much for him to bear.

Sabine felt her stomach flip and turned to look up at his face. He was smiling nervously as he looked back at her, his face flushed with the heat and the wine. She looked at him and let the feeling rush through her body, this was possible, it could work, it might work. It had to work.

She started to speak but was interrupted before she began.

The cabin door opened.

'Fuck me!' Galston said as he stomped the snow off his boots. 'Freeze a whores cunt oot there.' He spoke loudly. 'Whit you two up tae then?'

Craig looked around at the strange man filling the doorway to the cabin. The verbal intrusion was more shocking than the physical. 'What? Who are you?' he said.

Galston walked in and shut the door. He smiled and removed the woollen hat from his head, his hair was squashed and crazy. 'Hello everyone,' he said and picked up the half-filled bottle of wine to study the label. 'Nice.'

Craig's heart had started racing, who was this man? Here, far from anywhere with a Glaswegian accent talking in such a guttural and familiar fashion. He seemed to know him. 'Sorry, but I think you have got the wrong place, who are you?' He looked at Sabine. 'Can you go up to the restaurant and let them know.' He was speaking in a calm fashion, trying to not work up the man, not making direct confrontational eye contact. Keep him calm. Sabine was staring at the fire not moving.

'I dinnae fuckin think so, Craig,' Galston said replacing the bottle carefully. Craig's heart started racing as he mentioned his name. 'Naw, I dinnae fuckin think so,' he continued. 'You should have fuckin listened tae us a few weeks ago when we asked nice. Now ahm gonna ask properly an this time you will fuckin dae whit we say ok?'

It started to click in Craig's head but it didn't, he was in the Swiss Alps, far away from Scotland, far away from Orchid, far away from all of that. He shouldn't be here, couldn't be here.

'Look, let's talk about this, I'm not sure I know what you are talking about, but we can discuss whatever you want,' he said reasonably, repeating, 'Let's talk this over.'

'Aye ok. Let's dae that, Craig, lets go for a wee walk and talk aboot it.' He took Craig's glass and gulped the red wine down in one mouthful. 'Mon then. Get yer jaekit its fuckin cold oot there.'

Craig looked around the cabin, the fire, the debris from their dinner, he looked at Sabine still staring at the fire.

'I'll be back soon ok?' he said to the back of her head, but she didn't turn around.

'Hey, Sabine, he's talking with you, best you answer him,' Galston said sarcastically from the door, he was holding Craig's jacket out to him.

Craig's mind started working again. He knew her name, how could he know her name? He looked at Galston and then at Sabine.

'What the fuck is going on here?' he asked angrily. He was asking both of them and the words hung heavily in the thick warm air of the cabin.

'Just take yer jaekit and come on, will tell you all aboot it as we walk,' Galston said.

Sabine looked at Craig, her eyes were welling up. Craig looked back at her, angry. 'What is going on?' he repeated.

She didn't say anything and Galston grabbed his arm. 'She's a fuckin hoor ok, naw are you gonna come with me aer do ah have tae make ya?'

Craig kept looking at Sabine, a tear ran down her face and she mouthed sorry, silently. Craig shook his head. All the information was still being processed. She's a whore, what did that mean? He stared at her as his mind flashed over the last two days. A fabrication? It couldn't have been, it was real, it had to have been real. He looked at her and then took his jacket from Galston and made to leave the cabin. At the door he paused and turned to her. He wanted to say something to make her feel, to make her hurt. He wanted to see her react – he wanted to find out if she loved him as well – but she had her back to him.

'Fuck it,' he mumbled and then left. Walking out into the dark freezing night.

The door closed softly leaving Sabine alone in the cabin with the crackling fire and the remnants of a romantic dinner congealing on the plates.

She wept.

Outside Craig and Galston walked down the path towards the road. Their footsteps made a cracking sound in the frozen snow as they walked into the darkness.

Chapter 12

You cannot hide the sea. Even with the dark veil of a moonless sky it is there, pounding and growling. You can hear the breakers connect with the beach and feel their energy dissipate in the shale or sand, you can taste the air and the smell of it pervades everything. It swells and moves and will not be ignored even when it cannot be seen.

James stood staring out into the darkness feeling it a few steps in front of him. He imagined the expanse of dark water reaching to the horizon. He imagined ships, fishing boats, warships and tankers slowly working their way over the dark imaginary line. He let the images fill his mind. The ocean was a heavy object, unseen but very close. Like a planet silently passing by, close enough to touch, heavy enough to feel, but still invisible.

Behind him in the cottage Tony and Ewan were working on their prisoner. He could hear shouting and swearing but James preferred to stand outside and let them get on with it. The evening's events had caught up with him – he felt weak and tired. It was 2.43am. The wind clawed at his clothes. The rain had stopped but the storm was still lingering. He stood and stared into the darkness, his night vision was 100% but still he could see nothing. He couldn't remember a night darker than this. It was absolute.

The cottage was furnished in such an extreme minimalist fashion that Ewan doubted Tony had actually ever used it. A bed, a mattress, a fridge and a few wooden chairs was all it contained. It felt unused and unloved. In the nearly empty bedroom Dots was drowning. The panic reflex in his body was causing the cable ties to cut into the skin in his ankles and wrists. He bucked and strained against the bindings as he slowly drowned. Ewan held the cloth over his face and Tony poured the ice-cold water over it. Every time he breathed out Tony poured more to be certain he inhaled the liquid. Bubbles, froth and vomit worked through the fine holes in the muslin cloth as it was pulled tight over his face. They had stripped him naked and tied him to the metal frame of the bed. Tony then lifted the frame up and placed the bottom legs on the window sill resulting in him lying at an angle of 45 degrees, perfect for what he had in mind. He started by opening the window and pouring three buckets of the freezing liquid over his naked body, 'Just to get him in the mood,' he had told Ewan.

Ewan then did exactly as Tony instructed and watched with a morbid fascination as a human being drowned in front of him. He was amazed at the impact a piece of cloth and some water had on him; Dots bucked and stiffened against the cable ties, he retched and then choked on it, the panic in his body and his total being was clearly visible.

Ewan watched and willed him to die, he wanted them all to die, but of them all he wanted Dots and the other slim, young one to die first. They had visited him two months ago and he was terrified this would come out especially in light of James's accusations.

Tony worked from memory of an almost forgotten Army lecture and after twenty minutes of pouring the ice-cold water over the cloth their prisoner was ready to speak with them.

It was quicker than Tony remembered from the class but he knew very well the real world was often a very different place than a warm classroom and some projector slides. Dots' experience of interrogation resistance techniques was also non-existent. He capitulated fast and all three of them were relieved when he did.

Ewan removed the cloth and used it to wipe the vomit from his face. Dot's podgy white body was shivering, blood mixed with the wet thin hairs on his legs and his face, swollen and bruised from Tony's previous efforts, had lost the wild animal sneer. He was broken and had a resigned look about him. The blue and white 'Scotland the Brave' tattoo on his upper left arm was reduced to a pathetic smudge on his overweight, white body. There was no hiding place, the glare of the single bare 100W light bulb revealed everything.

'Go on then.' Tony stood holding the bucket, ready to resume in an instant.

He didn't have to.

* * *

Two years after setting up Orchid James and Craig had an issue. Not a big issue but an issue all the same, both Bingham and Holmes were essentially and for all intents and purposes, done. The only thing they had to do was check the bank account every so often and move the funds. There was always the risk of discovery but by then they had both accepted the risk, even James. Everything was automated, it was easy.

With Andreas's help Orchid had already gifted 100,000 mosquito nets to Southern Sudan and provided funding for two teachers for two years in a Malawi school. All in all, James and Craig were feeling justifiably smug. They travelled first class courtesy of Orchid, the company had purchased a small Alpine apartment and both of them were enjoying the supplementary income it generated.

Their issue was they were bored and had no idea what to do next.

Since they had successfully managed to tap into Bingham James had been working hard to shore up the gaps in the processes and to try to figure out a plan B. The fundamental issue with Orchid was it was illegal. Regardless of how benevolent, of how worthy it was, it was still theft. It was also theft on a pretty grand scale. At that point Orchid's multiple bank accounts had seen close to £2M flow through them. 'If we're discovered, we're fucked,' Craig told him cheerfully over a beer one Friday and he had to concede the point, he was right. They were fucked and he didn't like this at all so he spent his time trying to reduce the risk of this ever happening. Firstly he did the easy, logical things; some minor changes on the size and frequency of the payments would further minimise the risk of discovery. He also spent a lot of time understanding both company's internal controls and was unsurprised to find they were wholly inadequate. This didn't dissuade him though, a weak control environment could very easily be strengthened so he assumed they were strong and he studied, he investigated and he tweaked.

'Plan B?' James announced one evening.

Craig was sat sprawled on the couch of his newly acquired flat drinking beer from a bottle.

'Huh? What you talking about? Will you get a move on, I want to get out.'

Craig was staying over. His own house was far away from the city in Dunfermline and Susan had allowed him a pass for the evening. They were going out.

'No seriously, I think I have figured out a Plan B,' James said from the bathroom, he was buttoning up his shirt and running gel through his hair as he spoke.

'Ok, whatever, tell me about it later would you? Taxi'll be here any minute.'

Later that evening they were standing squashed into the corner of a bar.

'Go on then, Plan B?' Craig asked, he was less concerned about the risks and there was a hint of mocking humour in his voice.

'Ok, so we tell them,' James was grinning broadly.

'What?'

'We tell them,' he repeated.

'Tell who?'

'We tell Bingham or Holmes or whoever what we are doing.'

'Why? Ok look let me rephrase that. Why, *the fuck*, would we do that? Are you stupid?' He took a sip of his pint. 'This is your plan B? Fucksake, James, you really should stop worrying you know,' he added.

James was smiling.

'Listen to me will you? We tell them, we show them what the money has been used for, we brand everything appropriately. We announce it to them.'

'Go on.'

'We show them what the funds have been used for, we tell them this will be leaked and imagine the publicity they will get.'

He paused.

'You trying to tell me they are stupid enough to not understand how much good PR this would be for them? Do you know of a company who doesn't blow their own trumpet loudly every time they do anything mildly worthy? No, neither do I. This would be a coup for them, not only are they funding this shit, they are not shouting to the rafters about it, its priceless.'

Craig remained silent.

'Well?'

Craig took a gulp from his pint before responding. 'You know, it's not half bad, it might actually work. What if they don't go for it?'

'We tell them we release all the material we have been gathering.'

'What material?'

James just raised his eyebrows and laughed.

'Ahhh, *that* material. That works.'

'Yes.'

Their fundamental issue hadn't been resolved though. Who next? Both Craig and James worked for large global consulting firms. Both worked on implementing large ERP systems for European or global clients. James was the accountant, responsible for ensuring the financial modules worked according to the clients wishes. Craig was a programmer and adapted the off-the-shelf system to the specifics of the company, the country, or the business model the company required.

Their roles allowed them a unique insight into how a company runs its business and they designed the computer systems which track it, replicate it or account for it. From printing of invoices to producing internal accounts, between them they covered it. Bingham and Holmes were easy choices for them both, they deserved it. The issue was their current projects were not with similarly deserving companies and neither of them were ruthless enough to turn Orchid in the direction of an "innocent" company.

This is when they introduced Ewan to the company.

Ewan Gordon was someone James knew from early school, they were friends from primary school and had loosely kept in touch ever since. Like James, Ewan was also a chartered accountant and James knew he had recently joined a Braithswater Chemicals as their management accountant. Braithswater Chemical, in Craig and James's opinion, was a perfect candidate to become Orchid's third client.

A Canadian company Braithswater provided chemicals to heavy industry and in some instances governments. In the last ten years they had been responsible for two very high-profile chemical leaks and had been implicated in many more suspicious incidents. The company would pay the huge fines, apologise, but continue trading. Braithswater held tightly onto over 15,000 patents for products which significantly reduced cost in most heavy industries and it was these patents which enabled them to continue. They essentially created and owned the market and in doing so made sure the barriers to entry were extraordinarily high to dissuade any form of credible competition. In Scotland their largest customers were brewing and distilling.

If any company deserved to start taking their corporate social responsibilities more seriously it was Braithswater and they were very eager to start this process off for them.

'Let's have a chat with him then,' Craig said after James had run the idea past him.

'What do we tell him, I mean how much do we tell him?'

'If he is going to do it. Probably means we need to tell him everything.'

'Ok.'

James phoned Ewan the following morning and after a few beers and a lengthy discussion Ewan looked at him and took a large swallow from his pint.

'Ok.'

'What else do you need to know?' James asked, slightly surprised.

He just shrugged his shoulders and smiled.

'I dunno.' He drained his pint thinking. 'Whose round is it?'

* * *

Back in James's flat Galston woke, he had fallen asleep on the leather couch in front of the television. A heavy whisky glass sat on the table next to him. He sat up and looked around, remembering where he was. Two women in leotards were extolling the virtues of an ab-burner contraption on the television. His mouth felt dry and the stitches on his head throbbed. He ran his fingers along the scar and felt the raised ridge where the skin had been sewn together. It was lumpy and sore to touch. Standing up he killed the television and walked through to the bathroom. All the lights were on in the flat. Under the harsh strip light in the long thin bathroom he studied his face in the mirror. He looked old. He knew this. His beard and hair accentuated the aesthetics. He pulled his hair back and studied the scar. It was red and angry. Fuckin bitch, he thought to himself as he moved over and stood at the toilet. As he urinated he thought about the evening's events, he would call Sandy in the morning to update him. It wasn't good but wasn't a disaster either. Clearly this bunch were not the stupid kids Sandy had made them out to be. Dots was a bit of a stupid cunt, but still he was tough as old boots. Galston had personally witnessed this and was still struggling in his head to arrive at a scenario which had him coming second best to this crowd. The English guy must have been the reason he thought. He must be helping them and he must be the reason Dots is probably in a ditch at this moment. So who is he? Galston wasn't too bothered about Dots, he had seen plenty come and go. It was the unknown factor he disliked and the English voice on the phone was definitely an unknown factor. He would phone Sandy in the morning for directions. He wasn't going to go start fucking around with kids or women until he got the ok from Sandy, and he knew from painful experience calling him in the middle of the night wasn't an option. He padded back to the living room and mulled over the whisky before knocking it back and pouring another.

* * *

'So what now then?' Ewan asked Tony. They were standing just outside the cottage. Dots was still tied to the bed inside. Tony had just brought James up to speed with the information they had managed to get out of their prisoner, which was disappointingly little, nor enlightening. Much to Ewan's relief. They now knew who was at the top, where he was, who the man was that had killed Craig and had a rough idea of the extent of their abilities and what they wanted. They hadn't managed to figure out how they had discovered Orchid but after a while conceded he probably didn't know and in any event at that point it didn't really matter. It had become a moot point. They had found out – that was all that mattered.

Tony looked at them both before he spoke. 'You know, I don't really know.' He paused. 'We have a choice to make here.'

'Which is?' James spoke.

'Well we either do what they say or we don't.'

'Yeh, I think we've got that, Tony,' Ewan said deadpan, he was getting agitated again. 'I think we all worked that one out some time ago, I was rather hoping for something other than that, you know? Plan C or D?'

'Well, within those two choices we have other choices.' Tony ignored the sarcasm in Ewan's voice. 'We could, for example, do exactly what they say and give them everything they want.'

'Which is?' James repeated.

'What?'

'What exactly is it they want? Do they want a bag full of money, do they want to have a payout on a regular basis or do they *really* want Orchid turned in their direction 100% and we end up working for them?' James stared at his feet as he spoke.

'You know, James, that's exactly what I am trying to figure out. I don't really know. I'm assuming they want us, well you, to work for them. A bag full of cash might put out this fire for now but I don't think for a minute it'll make them go away.'

Ewan spoke, 'We could try, I mean for fuckssake guys, Craig has just been killed over this,' his words hung in the air. 'I'm willing to try anything.'

'Will they go after Sarah and the kids?' James asked.

Tony looked at his feet for a second pondering this question before staring at James and answering honestly, 'Probably.'

'Jesus Christ, Tony, offer them whatever they want. Give them whatever they want,' Ewan said.

'I agree, let's just do it, I mean look what happened to Craig, let's give them what they want and be done, this has to stop,' James was already resigned to his fate.

Tony paused before addressing them both. 'You know, I would tend to agree with you but there is one problem here.'

'Ok?'

'If you do this, you will be forever and I mean forever working for them, organised crime. You gotta realise this. This isn't a one-time deal with a start and a finish. No, this will go on and they will escalate it, push it.'

Ewan spoke, 'So what do you suggest Tony?'

'I suggest we try, at least try to compromise, let's meet them, let's give them a bag full of money, let's try to negotiate with these fuckers before you go and sell your souls to the Devil.'

Both Ewan and James nodded at this. James spoke, 'At least it might delay the inevitable.'

'Exactly,' Tony replied. 'And give me some time to work on a plan C.'

'Ok, what now?' Ewan asked.

'I need to make some phone calls and will call the guy who did Craig later to suggest a meeting. James can you put your hands on,' he paused for a second thinking. '£1.5 Million? Quickly?'

'I don't know, I need to phone Switzerland to find out,' he paused, 'probably.'

'Ok good, do that.' Tony paused, deep in thought. It was a plan of sorts, not a good one but any plan was better than no plan.

Ewan looked in the door of the cottage and then turned to them both. 'What about him?' he said, indicating towards the cottage and Dots who was still tied to the bed.

Tony spoke first. 'We'll dump him.'

'Dump him?' James questioned.

* * *

A radio alarm somewhere in the flat woke Galston, it was muffled but insistent and eventually he had to get up to find it. Light crept through the curtains as he walked around. He found it eventually on the windowsill of the main bedroom and the flat became silent again. He could taste the whisky from the night before and his head pounded with a mix of hangover and the scar throb. It was 7.30am.

At the same time, close to North Berwick, Dots stood at the side of the road trying to thumb a lift. Ewan and Tony had driven him to the main road then let him leave the car. He had sat in the backseat this time, quietly without a hint of the violence which had accompanied his arrival. He sat there and stared at the back of Ewan's head, Ewan could almost feel the eyes burning into his scalp. Ewan had sat there and waited for Dots to speak, to break the silence with a bombshell. He didn't, though, and just climbed out when told and shut the door calmly. Tony spoke with him at the side of the road before they pulled away to return to the cottage. Ewan just watched them and didn't ask Tony what it was they said, he would know if the information had been passed quickly enough. They had returned to the cottage and all sat down on the floor of the living room. James was asleep, Ewan rolled up his jacket and tried to do the same, Tony sat thinking as the sun came over the horizon, revealing the ocean in front of the cottage.

* * *

Three months previously Ewan lay in bed, sick. He had phoned his boss at 8am and in a croaky voice told him he would need to work from home that day. He wasn't sure if the hangover was hiding an underlying illness or if it was just 100% hangover. In either event he had thrown up twice since 4am and felt feverish enough to make the call. Only tomorrow would he know for sure if he was really sick. His weekend had started on Friday and ended at 4am Monday morning. This he knew for sure. These were stakes in the ground which he could with certainty hang on to. The parts in between were a blur but he knew the start and the end, which for Ewan, was normal. It had started in the Grassmarket at 5pm on Friday and ended at 4am that morning, when she left. This was when he ran out of booze, cocaine and cash which meant she left. Having used his cashpoint limit for that day already he would have to wait until Tuesday to be able to withdraw anything and the shops he visited, apart from Oddbins, didn't normally accept Visa. Samantha certainly didn't but she did smile at him before leaving his small basement flat. She left him there, naked and five minutes away from throwing up. He pulled the duvet over his head and tried to go back to sleep, everyday life had started two hours ago and the noises from the street above kept him awake and ill.

He had a working doorbell, the electronic sort which played an awful jingle and this was why initially he didn't notice the banging on the door. He didn't recognise the thumping so ignored it and willed himself back to sleep. Better to sleep it off than endure it awake.

But the banging was insistent and eventually he had to get up. Like a cloud of midges around his head it irritated and he had to move, he had no choice.

'Alright! Ok!' he shouted, muttering 'wankers' under his breath as he wrapped a towel around his bulging waistline and padded barefoot to the door. Through the centre glass pane he could see two figures. He opened the door. Two men stood there, an older fat one and a younger thinner one. The fat one grinned at him.

Everyone has things they regret in life, everyone wishes they had done something different. 'If I had my time again...' Everyone makes a mistake and regrets it. Everyone has guilt and everyone has a reason to feel guilty. To err is to be human. And as Ewan opened the door squinting against the daylight that morning, wearing only a towel he didn't know it but he was just about to be very human indeed.

He knew eventually his actions would have consequences but by that point he had all but forgotten about Maria. They reminded him and stepped inside for a "chat". It didn't take long before he gave them what they asked for. Who's involved? How do you do it? He used layman's terms of course, they wouldn't fuckin get it anyway he assumed. He could have told them anything. But he didn't.

* * *

'It's Gal,' Galston said. He had waited until 8am to phone Sandy, he couldn't wait any longer and figured this wasn't an unreasonable time to be phoning.

'The fuck dae you want?' Sandy responded sleepily, 'Dae you know wha time it is?' he added.

Galston ignored the question. 'Need tae talk, Sandy, things have gotten a little fucked up overnight.'

'Fucked up?' Sandy sat up in bed.

Galston then proceeded to give him the highlights of the night's happenings. It wasn't a pleasant conversation.

'So should I?' Galston asked, referring to his threat with the kids.

Sandy paused for a long time, his breathing was audible down the phone line. Eventually he sighed, 'You know, Gal, in aw the time a have known you…' He paused 'Naw. Dinnae. Call them again n arrange a meeting. Ah'm getting tae old for shite like that.' He hung up abruptly and Galston held the phone to his ear until the disconnected tone started. He stood up stretched and then walked into the kitchen in search of coffee.

He suspected he wouldn't be disappointed and wasn't.

* * *

Jacques Bertrand sat looking out over the dockyard. He had just finished his weekly check-in with his brother in London and was now sipping his second cup of black coffee. Once a week, every week, for the last eight years Jacques checked in with Jerome, at a pre-arranged place, online. By necessity it was the only contact they had but it set both their minds at ease. Pretty soon Jacques would join up with Jerome and after such a long time waiting it couldn't come soon enough for him. Marseille docks is a dirty place and Bertrand would have no remorse driving away from it all. He watched as heavy goods vehicles slowly backed up to the offload/load point a few hundred meters from a large container ship. Bertrand had always enjoyed early mornings. Mornings were industrious times of the day. Work got done in the morning, real work. As the day progressed industry would slow down, it was human nature to work in conjunction will the ebb and flow of the moon and sun. Everything slowed down as the day went on, but the morning was the time to work. He watched a lorry reverse away from the loading dock, its reversing alarm barely audible in his first floor office. It was heavy, the load sat lower down on the axles in contrast to the lorries queuing to load up. Jacques had a lot on his mind but never let his focus detract from the job in hand. He sat watching the lorries come and go for an hour before he saw the truck. He watched it pull up, he watched the driver jump out and speak with the loading foreman. He pointed to a pallet and then climbed back into the cab. Fifteen minutes later the truck pulled away from the dock, and Jacques sent a SMS to the Moroccan. He wouldn't miss him either.

Once he received the agreed standard SMS response he turned his attention back to his computer. A month ago, once he got the message from Jerome, he had started calling in the long list of debts. Some were easy and paid up or returned the favour, thanking him for his patience. Others were a little more problematic and would require a certain amount of persuasion. He looked at the spreadsheet in front of him. It was a simple list of names, numbers and dates. There was no commentary, this part remained in his head. Sandy Milne's name was on the list with a six-figure sum in the column next to it. He scanned further down the list and picked up the phone to call in another favour.

* * *

The sun broke through the thick clouds and shafts of light lit up spots on the ocean. The wind had dropped and the white foaming breakers merged together to form a large swell. Seagulls were the first to notice the respite and shrieked with excitement as they swooped and dropped down to the beach to pick through the storm debris. Inside the cottage three men slept. Curtains were another optional extra Tony had forgone and the three men were illuminated by the bright morning sunlight as they lay crumpled on the bare floorboards.

It was Ewan who woke first, he stood up stiffly and looked around the room. He drank some water from the tap and then went to find the toilet. When they were all awake Tony spoke.

'Ok, I am going to start making some phone calls, can you two head up and get some food and coffee? There's a BP garage five miles back up the road.' He passed James the keys to his car.

When they left he phoned Melissa from his own mobile. She would be worried and he spun her a story about a break-in at a factory he was managing. It seemed to work. He then picked up Dots' phone and dialled the number from the call log the night before.

The phone rang and startled Galston who was watching television and drinking his third cup of coffee. Dots' name flashed on the phone.

'Hello,' he said cautiously, not sure who would be on the other end.

'Ok, I have a solution,' Tony spoke as he watched Ewan and James pull away from the front of the cottage.

It was the English guy again. Galston was certain Dots was dead at this point.

'Where's Dots?' he asked.

'Fuck off, I couldn't give a shit about Dots or whatever his name is. I have a solution which should keep you happy, or at least keep your boss Sandy happy,' Tony replied: purposely dropping the name in.

It registered with Galston but he ignored it. 'You have a solution? Fuckin hope it's a "dae what we say" solution.'

'I have a solution ok?' Tony then went on to propose a meeting, just the two of them to start. At the cafeteria inside the Scottish Museum 5pm today. The cloak and dagger stuff made Galston smile.

'Aye right, whatever ya want. Nae sure what you want tae propose though, it's pretty simple from ma side. They dae it or ah start removing body parts fae small people.'

Tony winced at this but continued, 'You need to listen to me first, face to face. Do not touch them until we have spoken. I know you have people watching them so we won't try anything. Just meet me ok?'

Galston nodded "ok". He didn't have anyone watching them but didn't say anything, let him think anything he wanted.

Tony hung up and then picked up his own phone. He dialled two numbers from his phone book. When done he went through to the bedroom and cleaned up the mess from the night before, replaced the mattress on the frame and closed the door. He checked his watch, 9am, James would need to call the bank when he returned. He felt happier, he had a plan. It wasn't the best plan but any plan was better than no plan. He just hoped James could get the money fast.

James and Ewan returned with coffee and food. Their trip in the car was notable only for the lack of conversation, they journeyed in silence. Neither wanted to pick up where they left off the night before. Tony walked them through his plan. They ate, drank and asked questions. Tony noticed a change in them both, food and a plan seemed to have lifted their spirits. When he'd finished, he stood there looking at them both. 'Well?'

Ewan looked at James.

'Let's get going then,' he said.

James started refitting the battery to his mobile phone and Tony went to the car to retrieve a change of clothes and a toothbrush. He thought for a second and then went back in.

'You both look like shit. There's a Tesco in North Berwick and we have time. Go up there and get something clean to wear. James, can you clean that crap from your face before you go?' he said, referring to the black dried blood stuck to his face.

James nodded and put the phone to his ear. 'Andreas Rogenmoser, please,' he said business-like into the phone.

Ewan walked to the small bathroom to check his own face.

Chapter 13

Jacques replaced the receiver and returned to the list. He put a question mark next to Sandy's name and six-digit number. He disliked the Scotsman but had never had issues over the ten years they had done business. Jacques didn't need to like someone to do business with them. If they paid, Jacques would do business and up until six months ago the Scotsman had always paid. The mark-up his customers could add to his wholesale prices were sufficient to keep them paying and, importantly, keep them coming back. Normally there wasn't an issue but this particular customer had become an issue. Now that he was so close to getting out he had also become very sensitive to risk; pulling in another favour to recover what he could from the Scotsman was a risk but a risk he was still willing to take for close to a million euros. He scratched his head and stared out over the busy dockyard.

Across town in a small nightclub Gerald Fournier was sitting on a barstool. The club had been shut for three hours and the cleaners had just left. The place smelled of heavy-duty cleaning products. He had been drinking coffee and preparing to go home when the phone rang, he picked it up irritated but his tone changed immediately when he recognised Jacques voice. Once the call was over he sat surveying the small dance area surrounded by quiet intimate booths and then picked up the phone again to call his brother Michel. They had a job to do and this was one they couldn't screw up.

'Micha, its Gerald, we're going on a trip,' he said into the receiver.

* * *

Galston closed the door to James's flat carefully. He pushed the wooden splinters back into place and pulled the handle. He had showered, brushed his teeth and even found some painkillers in the bathroom cabinet. He felt good. The sun was breaking through the clouds and the throb in his head was starting to subside. Yes, things were looking up, and he was actually looking forward to finding out what the English guy had to offer. He had no apprehension about meeting him. He was intrigued and smiled to himself as he thought about the meeting place. The real world didn't work like the movies. Galston knew this. It's a very different place but clearly this man had watched more than his fair share. This would be fun, he thought, as he stepped out of the close and lit a cigarette.

* * *

James pulled into the supermarket car park, it was half-empty and seagulls swarmed over the overflowing crates and rubbish that littered the empty spaces. They had both cleaned themselves up as best they could but both still looked like two men who had been up all night in the rain fighting. The bright seaside sunlight accentuated the look. They were out of place and there wasn't anything they could do about it. They walked through the supermarket entrance and straight to the clothing section. Having something to do had had a positive effect on the two of them. James's outburst the previous evening was consigned to unmentionable box for the time being. Inside the supermarket the security guard watched them closely and shadowed them through the store. Earlier James had spoken with Andreas. The funds could be transferred immediately, this wasn't an issue. He had told James about the risks that additional transfers could pose and transfers for such large sums could potentially be watched. James knew this already but, given the circumstances, he really didn't have an alternative. The cash would be in the Orchid account later today. Actually putting his hands on the cash and filling a bag with it would be somewhat trickier though. Banks don't tend to let people walk in and withdraw £1.5M in cash just like that. Even though it was James's cash, he would still need to go in and explain why and have three forms of identity with him before they would hand it over.

* * *

Fifty minutes later Tony pulled the car off the small cottage track onto the main road and pressed the accelerator hard to the floor. They had a lot to get done before the meeting in the museum.

At the same time Galston was heading West on the M8, back to Glasgow to meet Sandy and in Marseille two brothers sat in a taxi heading to the airport. They had managed to get themselves booked on a scheduled flight to London's Gatwick airport the same day.

* * *

In the snowy mountain town of Interlaken Switzerland a young woman sat up in bed. The scars and bruises on her face had started to fade. She couldn't move properly, but knew this was due to her right leg being held tight in plaster. It felt heavy and she wondered how it would feel without the tightness covering the limb, something she had never experienced. She had been in the hospital for some time but for all intents and purposes it could have been forever. Her memory loss was total. The past month was clean and clear but before this there was nothing, just a dark, black wall. The hospital was her life and the routine became her normality. According to the nice young doctor who visited her at least twice a day she had been found next to a mountain road by some skiers. She had been the victim of an attack, this was obvious. Her right leg was broken, her face had been beaten badly and she had sustained five stab wounds to various parts of her body. Basically she had been left for dead the young man had told her solemnly. Miraculously none of the stab wounds were life-threatening and a beating, however painful, is rarely fatal. Hypothermia was the most dangerous aspect of her condition but the team at Spital Interlaken were very well trained in hypothermia. They worked hard and the young woman survived. A month later she had virtually recovered and, apart from a few nasty scars and the leg plaster, was in surprisingly good health. The police, however, were confounded. She carried no ID and there was no obvious reason for the attack. They had searched the area intensively but it seemed she must have been moved to where she was found, away from wherever the attack took place.

The medical team had notified the police when she arrived and once she was stabilised started working through the usual medical checks. There was some trace of alcohol in her system indicating she had been drinking the night before, no drugs of any form. She had engaged in sexual activity within twenty-four hours of being found. Traces of semen were found and this provided the police with a potential DNA lead. A young pretty woman, found naked, beaten, stabbed and left for dead. Add to this sexual activity and alcohol and Thomas Gasser, the lead investigator, had a working hypothesis: Young girl on a date, drinking alcohol and the date turns nasty when she refuses her suitors advances. Unable to deal with her refusal, he flies into a rage, beats, stabs and rapes her and then disposes of the body. Thomas was experienced enough to be aware the dangers of sticking to one hypothesis, but since she had been brought in and they had found the semen they had not advanced a single step. No progress at all. He was going with his hypothesis until something else turned up to prove him wrong.

An attempted murder and rape in Interlaken is rare but even in such a small mountain town the excitement starts to dull after such limited progress. After a month the case inevitably dropped down their priority list. Their only remaining hope was for the young girl to regain her memory and then they could start asking some real questions.

This, according to the team at the Spital could be tomorrow, next week, next month or never.

She felt strong. She was ready to go home, her body was ready. The problem for Sabine Weinstrom was remembering where exactly home was?

* * *

'So whit dae ya think he wants?' Sandy asked Galston, they were standing in the kitchen of Sandy's house. Sandy was making them both coffee.

'Dunno, ahm guessing he will want tae offer us something. Money probably, tae fuck off.'

Sandy pressed the plunger down on the cafeteria and poured them both a cup.

'Whit dae you think, Gal? They're worried, right? They fucking should be. Ah saw the video.' He turned to face him. 'Oh magic there by the way, that cant've been easy.'

'It was fuckin cold maer than anything Sandy an this is a total bitch,' Galston said, pointing to the scar on his head.

'Aye, well, tae be expected ah guess. We're nae accountants mind? Anyways, ah think you should go. If they offer money an it's enough, let's take it the now.' He paused and sipped the coffee. 'We can always gae back, speak with them again.'

This was unlike Sandy. Once Sandy had a plan, a strategy, he would follow it without deviating. In a lot of cases even when it had become clear it wasn't working. This was Sandy, the way he was and he was the boss.

'Ok, wanna tell me how much is enough?'

Sandy ran his hand through his white hair thinking. He had this issue with the fuckin Frenchy which would blow up sooner or later.

'£2M. They willne be able tae get it. So take half that the now and get another million in a month.'

'Ok,' Galston had his orders.

'Whit dae ya think Gal, am ah getting soft in ma old age?' Sandy asked.

Galston instantly thought about the night in the Alps.

'Naw, Sandy, you're nae getting soft,' he shook his head.

Sandy was relaxed here. This was more the Sandy his wife and children knew, the soft smiling granddad Sandy. Galston felt uncomfortable with this version of his boss. He knew the real Sandy, the spitting, snarling, plotting and murdering Sandy. At least the one he knew was real, he thought.

'Perhaps am no. Tell me Gal, how daed that bitch manage tae dae that tae ya anyway, big tough guy like you?' he said smiling, adding, 'Ya didnae try tae fuck her did you, Gal?'

Galston ignored this and finished his coffee.

'Will head off then,' he said, placing his cup in the dishwasher.

'Phone me once you've met him. An try tae find out what happened tae Dots eh? Dinnae want his stinking body turning up.'

'Aye right.' Galston picked up his jacket and left the house, it was midday, plenty of time to get back to Edinburgh.

* * *

James pushed open the door to the Royal Bank of Scotland private-banking section and walked up to the young receptionist. Her light pine desk was an effective barrier, professional but clearly designed as a first line of defence. Behind her was a bank of doors, modern and hazed to offer privacy for the banks more special customers. A glass lift moved upwards towards the second floor. James knew that even in personal banking there was a hierarchy. He also knew that he would be taken to the second floor given the size of the transaction and the size of Orchid. The second floor was reserved for the customers the bank could not afford to lose. The bank had a similar ambience to the Alt-Yverdon. It just felt cheaper. A plastic version.

'Hi, James Bisset to see Mr Grant, I have an appointment at 12.30.' He smiled politely as he spoke.

She smiled back, moved the mouse and found the appointment.

'Ok, Mr Grant will be down shortly, do you want to wait over there?' She indicated to a pair of leather seats in the corner. 'Can I get you something to drink, tea, coffee, water.'

'No thank you,' James said as he sat down.

* * *

Just around the corner Tony and Ewan were sitting in a small coffee shop waiting for him. They had rehearsed and Tony had spent some time cleaning James's face up. By the time he walked into the bank his face was a little puffy but there was little to show for the night's activities. He wore light khaki trousers and a black, unbranded polo shirt. He looked exactly like they had hoped – a professional man on his day off. They bought a small black executive trolley bag from the railway station and he left them there. They sipped their coffee in silence, nervously waiting for him to return.

* * *

James stood up when he saw Cameron Grant approach. They had met on a couple of occasions, always within the confines of the private-banking building. Cameron smiled as he approached.

'Mr Bisset, good to see you again, how are you?' he said offering his hand.

'Very good thanks, Cameron, and you?' James replied shaking his hand.

They walked towards the lift side by side and Cameron spoke quietly, 'Good to see the weather's improved, I hear it's going to be fine for the weekend.' Business or banking was never discussed outside of the private rooms in this section of the bank. They covered banal topics as they stood in the lift and walked through the quiet corridor to the designated meeting room. Once inside and James had refused another offer of refreshments Cameron spoke, 'So you have arranged to make a withdrawal today, in cash, £1.5M,' he said looking at a piece of paper in front of him.

'Yes, that's right,' James replied, without offering anything further.

'Ok, well, you know this is not a usual transaction and due to the money laundering laws I do need you to answer a few questions before I can legally carry out the transaction?'

'That's fine,' James said, relaxed. 'I don't really want to have that much cash on my person either but I have this particular client, well...' He paused. 'He is quite particular, and frankly after the last few years has lost his trust in banks.' James smiled as he said that.

Cameron laughed. 'Yes, I can understand that, what does he do with it? Under his mattress?'

James laughed as well. 'You know, I am not sure but I think he buys gold, Austrian Mint gold bars I think. I believe he flies into Vienna with a briefcase stuffed with money and buys them there and then.'

They both laughed and then Cameron turned serious. 'Ok, so hang on, let me pull this questionnaire up and we can get it done. Oh, before you do, I presume this is Sterling right?' James nodded. 'Ok, and what denomination do you want it in, I presume largest notes?'

James pointed towards his trolley bag. 'It needs to fit in there,' he said, grinning.

Cameron looked over and picked up the phone and started giving instructions. After he was done he turned back to James. 'It won't fit in that, even if we do £50 notes it's still going to be too much, I have asked for my security team to provide you with two briefcases and we'll set the combination for you. Do you want security to accompany you? It's probably safest.'

James shook his head. 'Its ok, my car is outside and I meet my client in thirty minutes, I won't be walking around with that much cash, trust me.'

'Ok, let's get on with this then – so firstly, where has the funds come from? I will need to see source bank accounts,' he added.

For the next ten minutes James answered the questions with the answers he had prepared. If the transaction was to be scrutinised in any depth it would fall down, but it was good enough to get the cash and at that point that was all he cared about.

Twenty minutes later James walked out of the bank carrying two very heavy silver briefcases, combination locks set to his year of birth. He walked out into the sunlight and turned right back towards the café.

Tony and Ewan saw him approach and stood up to leave. They met him on the street.

'Any problems?' Tony asked.

James held up one briefcase. 'Carry this would you, weighs a ton, £750,000 each.'

Tony took it. 'Always wondered what this amount of cash would feel like,' he said absently, then started walking down the street towards the multi-story car park. James and Ewan followed him.

'Shame we have to give it away,' Ewan said to no one in particular.

'Let's see shall we?' Tony said, without stopping or breaking stride.

Chapter 14

BD452 Marseille to Gatwick cleared the low cloud covering Southern France with a slight judder. It was thirty minutes delayed due to the congestion at Gatwick but with a strong tailwind the pilot was confident he would make up most of the time. As the plane levelled off, the seatbelt sign disappeared and the passengers visibly stretched out. Seats were reclined, laptops opened and a small queue formed for the lavatory. Gerald and Michel Fournier were seated towards the rear of the plane, Michel in the middle seat, Gerald the window. A fat Asian man completed their row.

Michel fished in his bag for his headphones and Gerald stared out at the brilliant blue sky through the plastic bubbled window. 'You ever been to Scotland?' he asked his brother.

Michel nodded his head. 'I went to Edinburgh with Jeanine two years ago.'

Gerald nodded. 'And?'

'And what? It was a holiday, we took pictures and fucked a lot.'

Gerald smiled. 'Nice place?'

Michel shrugged his shoulders. 'Cold,' he said and placed the earphones in his ears breaking off the conversation.

Ten minutes later he took the earphones out again.

'Are we going to Edinburgh?'

'No, Glasgow,' his brother replied turning from the window

'Why are we doing this, Gera?'

Gerald looked back out at the blanket of puffy white clouds far below, it stretched as far as the horizon. He looked back at his brother. 'Because the Fournier's always repay a debt and we owe Bertrand.'

'Do we? Why?'

'Trust me on this, Micha, just trust me, we do.'

'Ok,' he replied replacing headphones. Gerald turned back to the view and let his mind drift over the plan he had thrown together in the few hours since Bertrand had phoned him. They were to drive to Glasgow from London stopping off in Manchester along the way to pick up supplies. He had already phoned his contact there so knew they would be ready. He had the Scotsman's address. The plan was a simple one, go there and persuade him to repay the debt. If he couldn't be persuaded, kill him, and take what they could. Gerald didn't plan on staying any longer than necessary in Scotland. He wanted to be back home within two days, no longer. They would reach Glasgow by late that evening. Tomorrow morning they would visit the Scotsman and then head south again. Gerald had booked return flights for next week. They wouldn't be using them. They would return overland. Drive to London and take the train from there. It was safer that way. He stared out of the window feeling good. It was a good plan, simple and easy. He and his brother had done this many times before so he had no reason to be anxious. His mind moved to the Scotsman, someone who up until this morning he didn't even know existed, Sandy Milne. He studied the picture which had been dropped off just after receiving the phone call. The photo was good, very clear, almost too good. According to the courier it was also very recent. He stared at the old man in the picture and wondered if he could be persuaded. He hoped so. Gerald had an inherent dislike of violence. It was a necessary evil but in his mind something to be used only as a last resort. First and foremost Gerald was a businessman. His brother on the other hand tended to think of violence as the first and only resort. So when Gerald failed, Micha would step in. And Micha, as he had witnessed many times, could be very persuasive.

The captain interrupted his thoughts and he sat there listening to a clipped British accent talk about headwinds, cabin safety and arrival weather. Below him Europe was just one big continuous blanket of cloud. Gerald idly watched it pass by, his mind drifting over his plan, trying to find flaws.

* * *

4.15pm: Galston parked up in a hotel car park. He checked his watch. Early. He pushed back the seat and stretched his legs. His head throbbed so he closed his eyes and tried to imagine how the meeting would go. He wasn't worried. He didn't anticipate anything kicking off, given the conversations, and the chosen location, but he knew from experience to come prepared. He pulled the bayonet from its sheath. It glistened in the dull light and the blade felt smooth to touch. A light sheen of oil lined the dark metal blade. It felt familiar, its weight and hatched metal handle. He held it in his hand and closed his eyes again, letting his mind drift.

* * *

4.35pm: Tony parked the car in the public car park around the corner from the museum. Switching off the ignition he turned to Ewan and James.

'Ok, I am going to go in. I don't think anything will happen but if I am not back by.' He paused. '5.30, leave, go get the girls and fucking disappear ok?'

They both nodded.

'Take that,' he said, indicating to the cases, 'and fuck off somewhere ok.'

'We got it Tony, 5.30, you're not here, we fuck off, it's fine,' James said.

Tony looked at them both. 'Fine.'

'It will be ok you know? We will deal with this today. We will stop it today and go back to whatever the hell we consider normal life is.' He paused and looked around. 'Ok, I'm off.' He left them in the car.

* * *

4.50pm: Galston and Tony entered the museum at the same time. Tony held the door open for the older man and they walked together towards the café situated in the heart of the museum. People milled around talking in hushed tones as they took photographs and wandered amongst the statues and works of art. A group of Asian tourists all wearing the same cheap, white and red jackets and holding electronic guides to their ears, approached them. Tony paused to let them past, Galston continued walking, forcing them to split as he headed on to the café. As he waited for the group to pass, Tony glanced around the main hall of the museum. Standing pride of place was a full skeleton of a Tyrannosaurus Rex, three kids were running around its base making roaring sounds and giggling. He looked up at the million-year-old predator and smiled. A monstrous beast which once roamed the earth hunting its prey, no thought or consideration for who or what it hunted. It was a simple-minded animal with only one thing on its mind, no conscience. He looked over the skeleton and tried to imagine the bones covered with thick flesh, tried to imagine its eyes darting around, its small almost deformed upper limbs moving erratically, out of sync with its powerful legs. He wanted to see the head move, turn quickly and then the 3-metre-tall monster break free scattering tourists and children in its wake.

The last of the tourists passed and he continued following the cup and saucer signs towards the café. It was in the basement and as he entered he noticed Galston immediately. The café was empty apart from one family, Galston wasn't difficult to spot. He instantly recognised him as the man who entered the building with him. He walked towards Galston, studying the man. He pegged him at about sixty years old and even seated he could see he was powerfully built. He was big but not fat, not muscular either, the sort of man who contained a hidden blunt trauma

strength. Tony had met many like him in the past. Simplest way
to deal with men like this was to avoid them which given their
size wasn't normally too difficult. Never stand toe to toe with
them. That would be a mistake.

He sat down opposite and smiled.

'That looks nasty,' he said pointing at the scar on Galston's
head. 'I really fucking hope that was Craig.'

Galston smiled back. 'Walked intae a door.'

'Right.'

'So you set this up, what dae you want?' Galston asked and
sipped his coffee.

'You didn't get me coffee? That's not very nice.'

Galston just looked at him.

'What dae you want?' he repeated.

'I want you and your lot to fuck off.' He waited as the family
walked by and then continued. 'I want you to fuck off immediately.'

'Why would we dae that?' he replied, shaking his head.

'Because I am going to give you a bag full of money and if you
don't accept it, I will fuck you over, like we did to your friend.'

Galston paused for a second thinking this over. 'Where daed
you dump him?'

'Why?'

'Because ah dinnae want his fat carcass turning up stinkin the
place down.'

'Nice, good to see you look after your own.'

Galston ignored this. 'Why dae you think we wouldnae take
yer money an then just carry oan?'

'Because I trust you.'

'You trust us?' he said raising his eyebrows.

'Of course I don't fucking trust you, fucking idiot.' Tony
looked around the deserted café, there was a young female
leaning on the counter waiting for them to leave.

'No, I am offering the money as a means to get you to fuck off nicely, if you don't, I *will* make you fuck off.' He paused and smiled a thin smile. 'Not so nicely.'

Galston smiled. 'Fair enough, how much?'

'One million.'

'You know, in another world ah might actually quite like you. You are so stupit it's quite endearing an naw that Dots has fucked off ah have a vacancy fur a team idiot.'

Tony didn't say anything, he just sat there staring at him.

'Two million.'

Tony leaned forward on the small café table 'We don't have two million, this isn't a bank you are robbing here you know? We have one and a half and that's all we have.'

'Where is it?'

'Not here.'

'Can fuckin see that,' he sighed and shook his head. 'Ok now you are starting tae bore me, one and a half, fine, bring it tae this address tomorrow morning 9.30. Bring the other two fuckwits with you,' he passed over a slip of paper and stood up.

'Why bring them?' Tony asked looking up at him.

'Because ma boss wants tae say hi tae them.' He then walked out of the café leaving Tony alone.

Tony gave it two minutes then stood up and left. He smiled at the girl as he passed. Outside in the main hall the tourists had all but left, he strode across the hall, his shoes clicking on the polished floor. He didn't even glance at the million-year-old predator as he passed it. It stood there passively. Silent and impotent.

* * *

Gerald pulled the small hire car into the parking space in the motorway service station. Sanjay had given him the location just off the M6 near Oldham. He told his brother to wait by the car and then walked towards the restaurant. It was 8.30pm and the restaurant was busy, there was a queue for the women's toilet stretching out into the main concourse. Children ran around burning up energy as their parents looked on wearily. Gerald was tired but there was still a long way to go. He scanned the restaurant and spotted Sanjay in the corner. Sanjay Agarawal was Gerald's UK contact. He never really knew what Sanjay did for a living other than supplying whatever it was he needed. Sanjay could get anything, he was discreet and reasonably priced therefore always in high demand. Perhaps this was his full time job Gerald thought as he approached the rake thin fifty-something-year-old Indian man.

'Sanjay!' he said holding out his hand.

Sanjay stood up and smiled, he shook the hand vigorously. There was a wiry strength in his skinny arms. He patted him on the shoulder.

'Gera, good to see you. You're late.'

'I know.' Gerald slid onto the plastic seat, 'Fucking English traffic.'

Sanjay nodded. 'Fancy anything?' he said indicating to the servery.

Gerald shook his head. 'No, can't, got Micha in the car and we still have a long way to go.'

'Where you going, Gera? What's this about?' Sanjay asked quietly.

Gerald just stared at him, not saying anything. Sanjay understood and knew well enough to not ask twice.

'Ok then, let's get it done,' he said cheerily as he stood up.

'Let me get a couple of your awful coffees first.'

They left the restaurant and walked to Sanjay's car. A rusty old Ford Escort. He opened the boot and inside was a cheap fake leather shoulder bag. He looked around then reached inside, unzipped the bag and stood back.

Gerald stooped down and studied the contents of the bag. Inside were two Beretta M9 9mm Pistols, a box of sixty rounds and two spring-loaded coshes. He quickly checked one of the handguns, removed the fifteen round magazine, pulled the slide back, checked the barrel and pulled the trigger. It gave a satisfying click. He replaced the gun and zipped up the bag.

'Happy?' Sanjay asked.

'I'm always happy, Sanjay,' Gera replied and shook his hand adding, 'Thanks.'

'Good luck, eh? And say hi to Micha for me,' Sanjay said before closing the boot and getting back into the car.

Gerald walked towards the hire car carrying the two Styrofoam coffee cups with the bag over his shoulder. Micha was standing beside the car smoking.

'Any problems?' he asked.

Gerald shook his head and passed over the coffee.

'When are we going to do it, Gera?' he asked sipping the hot, brown, flavourless liquid.

'Tomorrow morning.' He put the bag in the boot of the car.

* * *

'They want us there as well?' Ewan wasn't very happy and his tone reflected this. They were driving out of the city again.

'Yes,' Tony replied. 'They want to meet you and James.'

'Why?'

'I don't know why, they just do so we'll need to deal with it ok?'

'Fine let's get it done. Let's meet them, give them the money and go home,' James responded from the back seat, he was staring out of the window. The two silver cases were sat on the seat next to him.

'Where are we going now?' Ewan asked.

'Back to the cottage,' Tony said, not taking his eyes off the road, and sticking religiously to the speed limit.

James stared out of the car window and drifted off.

He was in a room. It was murderously hot, like the inside of an oven. A huge aircraft hangar of a room and he was walking across the expanse. Laughter was coming from the other corner and he squinted to see where it was coming from but couldn't make out anything in the darkness. He was sweating and his feet burned. It was as if the heat was flowing straight through his shoes. The hangar seemed to grow and the laughter wasn't getting any closer. He wasn't moving but he could see his feet moving. He started to run towards the sound. He had to see who it was. He sprinted, his feet grew hotter and hotter, sweat stuck his clothes to him and stung his eyes. He sprinted and then stopped suddenly. He saw who was laughing and recoiled at the sight. He tried to scream but no sound came out. Craig was sitting on a wicker chair laughing. His face a dull dark unearthly grey. He stood up on one leg and held onto the chair to steady himself. His other leg was no more than a stump, severed as it was above the knee. Blood flowed out and there was a large black puddle of blood stretching across the floor. The white-washed wall of the hangar had blood streaks and splatters. Chunks of flesh were everywhere. James wanted to run away but felt himself being pushed towards his dead friend. He tried to resist but his feet slipped on the blood and polished floor. He scrambled but was slowly forced forward. Craig's arm separated from the shoulder and started hanging by its veins only, it flopped as he moved. The grey face laughed deeply and then his old friend spoke in a gravelly, earth-filled voice. It was Galston's voice. 'Ya fuckin cunt, James. Ya ken it's Ewan, so whit ya fuckin fannying aroond fer?'

* * *

Later that evening they sat on the floor of the cottage, the wind was picking up again, whistling through the old building. The constant boom of the sea crashing against the beach was the only sound which made it through the noise. Plastic sandwich containers were strewn across the floor and they each sat sipping beer from cans.

'Will it just be us tomorrow, Tony?' James asked.

Tony munched on his sandwich. 'No, not tomorrow, tomorrow we'll have a little help.'

'Who?' James asked, suddenly interested in this information. Until this point Tony hadn't mentioned anything about help.

'A couple of friends will be there. Not in with us, but ready.' He didn't need to say why, this was obvious to everyone in the room.

'Who?' James repeated.

'Friends,' Tony said more directly. 'Just some friends ok? Can you both please just trust me now?'

Ewan and James fell silent.

Tony stood up and walked towards the bare kitchen. The wind rattled the window. He put his hand against the single-glazed window and stared out into the darkness.

'Ok, tomorrow might be a disaster, it might be.' He absently turned the taps on and off. 'It might be a disaster but you both need to trust me, I am doing everything I can to make sure it isn't.'

The cottage fell silent, no one spoke. No one had anything else to say. James and Ewan could push Tony to divulge all the details of his "friends", and his plan, but the truth was they didn't want to. Partly because they didn't want to take responsibility and partly because they wanted to trust Tony. Understanding the warts-and-all plan would be to understand the risk, and both Ewan and James were happy to remain ignorant.

Tony's "friends" were in fact one friend but this was something he felt best kept to himself. Brian Toshack, Tosh, was the friend and had been a friend of Tony for nearly fifteen years. Tony trusted him and knew what he was capable of. Since early that morning Tosh had been waiting for the call. He received it five minutes after Tony walked out of the museum café and was presently driving north from Liverpool, carefully. Tosh saw no reason to be stopped for anything stupid, especially since he was driving with a M40A5, 51mm, US-military sniper rifle in a bag, in the boot. He stuck to the seventy-mile-an-hour limit and listened to Talk Sport as he worked his way north.

* * *

At the same moment Micha and Gerald checked into their hotel. It was a cheap affair but neither brother complained. They had six hours before they were back on the road and all they were concerned about was a bed and a shower.

* * *

For Ewan and James the night would pass slowly. James's dreams became more violent and bloody as the night passed. Tony slept soundly on the floor covered in his jacket. Micha and Gerald snored. Sandy sat watching Newsnight and Galston sipped whisky staring out over the lights of a city he once knew intimately.

Chapter 15

Lochwinnoch is a small village ten miles west of Glasgow. Its proximity to the city and relative country aspect make it popular with commuters who enjoy the city and its benefits but want to escape the hustle and bustle. This popularity had driven up house prices in recent years and thus transformed what was once a farming community into a relatively wealthy village comprised of solicitors, accountants, doctors and the like. Sandy had lived just outside of the village for twenty years and had enjoyed its rise through the social hierarchy. As it moved up, so did Sandy. He was active within the community, sponsoring the local boys' football team and sitting on various community committees. To the village of Lochwinnoch, Sandy Milne was a pillar of the community, generous and likable. He was clearly successful in business. Even in the economic downturn Milne Security seemed to go from strength to strength and no one questioned this apparent bucking of the trend. Apart from his community activities Sandy generally kept himself to himself. He lived in a self-built house 2 miles from the centre of the village on land he had purchased from a local farmer and he thoroughly enjoyed its remoteness. It also allowed him to conduct business from home when needed.

Sandy's wife, Sammi, was aware of what he did for a living having been married to him for thirty years but did little to dissuade him. She enjoyed the fruits of his labour too much. So she simply ignored how he made his money. Currently she was on a week-long shopping trip to New York with her sister doing exactly that. Last year Sam had persuaded her husband to add a 40ft conservatory to the already extensive house and it was here he was sitting in his dressing gown sipping his morning coffee and reading the newspaper. It was 7.40am and the sun was just clearing the horizon diluting the dark night a dull grey. A steady drizzle fell and the wind had all but disappeared.

From a copse of trees some fifty metres away Tosh watched Sandy through the sight of his rifle. He had been in position for an hour. He had scouted the house as soon as he arrived. The conservatory seemed the most likely room but he was ready to move and adapt. He just hoped this would be the room. The light in the conservatory gave him a perfect line of sight and he knew even in full daylight at this distance, he would be all but invisible. He calculated the distance and set the range appropriately. A round released would cover the distance in less than 1/100 of a second, the weather conditions were good so no wind compensation would be needed. His only slight concern was the double-glazed glass surrounding the conservatory but there was nothing he could do about this and at such a short distance it wouldn't have much effect on the trajectory. He'd already decided to aim for the centre of the body mass. This would allow for an inch of skew and death would come just as certainly, albeit a little bit longer. Content, he set the weapon down and covered it with a towel. Rolling round, he pulled his cell phone from his pocket and sent an SMS to Tony and then lay on the damp grass in his green waterproofs and waited. It was cold and miserable but Tosh had many years' experience of this. For him waiting *was* his job or at least 9/10ths of it.

* * *

Tony, Ewan and James climbed back into the car. All were tired, miserable and anxious after a restless night and two days of being basically, on the run. They knew what had to happen to make it all stop but nobody was happy that they had to do this. Tony was equally anxious but had learned how to suppress it, how to push it aside. He pulled into the BP garage forecourt and they all got out. Nobody wanted to eat but Tony forced them.

* * *

Micha and Gerald left their cheap hotel and stood at their car studying the map, it wasn't far, about fifteen miles Micha estimated so they used the spare time to run through the plan once again. Gerald would go straight to the house while Micha would, as usual, examine the perimeter before joining him. This was probably too much caution under the circumstances but it was a process they always followed. It was a habit, and they were certain they were both still here today on account of these habits. Micha would check the perimeter and then join his brother in the house. By this time it would be clear which approach they should use to persuade the Scotsman. It was a good plan, a simple plan, a plan which would work.

* * *

Galston parked on the gravel drive outside Sandy's house and climbed out of the car. It was dreich but still took the time to stretch his legs and smoke a cigarette. He lit up and walked to the edge of the driveway looking up the slight incline over the manicured lawn. Beyond the regimented hedge the fields stretched off into the distance. In the centre of the field was a small copse of trees and he watched a couple of sparrow hawks swoop and dive above it hunting for food or carrying out a mating ritual – he didn't know which but it made for an impressive display and he idly watched them dance in the morning sky.

Uh oh, who are you? Tosh thought as he trained the scope on Galston and looked directly at him. He knew from experience that the man couldn't see him but through the scope they were making eye contact and no matter how hard he tried to ignore the feeling it still unnerved him. He held his forefinger across the trigger guard and watched the grey-haired old man smoke his cigarette in the damp. I could make you dead immediately, he thought, as the man flicked his cigarette away and turned towards the house. He followed him with the scope to the door. The old man knocked at the door and Tosh watched as the man in the conservatory stood up to answer the door. For a second they both disappeared from view and then reappeared in the conservatory. In his head Tosh had already named them; Old Bald Man and Old Man with Beard.

'Whit time they coming?' Sandy asked as they walked across the conservatory floor. It was warm inside the house and Galston followed his boss removing his jacket as he did.

'9.30am, I told him tae bring the other two as well. Thought you might wanna meet em,' he said as he flopped on a cushioned wicker chair throwing his jacket on the floor beside it.

Sandy nodded. 'Good idea, let's take the money faer now and then speak with them in a month or so.' He stood up again checking his watch, it was 8.50am. 'Coffee?' Galston nodded. 'You know where it is. Help yersel, ah need tae change.'

He left Galston alone in the conservatory. Galston sat there for a second then stood up looking around. The birds were still dancing above the copse and for the briefest of moments the thought that they might be spooked flashed through his mind before he dismissed it and walked towards the kitchen and the coffee machine. His head still throbbed and silently he cursed the kraut whore, again.

* * *

'We ready for this?' Tony asked, turning in his seat to face them. They had parked up in the village opposite a small corner shop.

'I am,' James replied from the backseat. He was sitting as usual with the two silver cases of money next to him.

Ewan nodded from the front passenger seat.

'Ok, look I have a guy watching the house, he's already there.'

He paused to see a reaction. There was none so he continued, 'He's there just in case. If you see me raise my right arm, drop to the floor.'

'What?' Ewan asked.

'My right arm, like this,' he raised his right arm against the roof of the car.

'I know what your right arm is, Tony. Was just wondering why that is the signal, why not an ear piece or a normal signal of some sort.'

'Ewan, it doesn't matter what the signal is so long as it's something unusual, something you wouldn't expect me to do ok? It's my right arm.'

'Ok,' James said. Ewan was smiling and considering the circumstances both James and Tony smiled as well.

'Why not unzip yourself instead?' Ewan said. 'That'd be unusual.'

'He needs to be able to see the signal Ewan,' James said instantly. They all laughed at this and for the briefest of moments the tension in the car reduced. It was male pub banter, it was how it used to be. How it was before Craig. Tony turned the key in the ignition and pulled the car away from the curb.

* * *

Galston looked at his watch again, 9.25am. They should be arriving now, and then he heard the crunch of tires on gravel. He turned to Sandy, now dressed in jeans and a dark roll neck sweater, 'Ready fae this?'

'Fuck off, Gal, gae welcome our guests.'

Tosh watched the car arrive. He knew it was Tony from their conversation the day before. He watched them climb out of the car and named the two passengers; Fat and Thin. The door opened and they all trouped inside. Thin was carrying two brief-cases and judging from his stiff-legged gait they were heavy.

Galston just nodded at them to follow him inside. Once inside the conservatory they stood awkwardly. Tony could see the copse behind the conservatory and hoped this was where Tosh had managed to get himself set up. It would be perfect but neither had had the luxury of any sort of real reconnaissance.

Galston turned to James. 'Why the fuck daed ya run, fuckin twat?'

Tony stepped over purposely between James and Galston. 'Why don't we just deal with what we have to deal with and get it over ok?'

They stared at each other, both smiling for a brief second before Sandy spoke. 'Calm a fuck down right. Yer both tough guys ok? He's right, let's aw have a quick chat and we will aw be on our way.' He indicated to the cases next to James. 'That what ah think it is?'

James nodded and Sandy walked over and picked one up. 'Wow, heavy,' and then noticing the combination lock asked for it. James gave him the combination. Sandy placed the case on the coffee table and worked the lock combination. 'Galston, gae get our guests some drinks will you?' he said as he opened up the case.

* * *

Tosh was watching the exchange intently through the scope, he watched Tony and Old Man with Beard squaring up, he watched Old Bald Man take one of the cases and watched Fat and Thin stand at the back of the room. The safety was off, his finger resting on the trigger and his breathing regular. He was 100% focused on the conservatory and Tony. His world was reduced down to the scope and his breathing. He focus was absolute and didn't notice or hear the small hire car pull up alongside the hedge at the end of the driveway. He didn't notice Micha jump over the hedge and start running, half crouched in his general direction, zigzagging through the knee height scrub grass. Tosh had the cross hairs trained firmly in the centre of Old Bald Man's chest, he was now the closest to Tony and Fat and Thin. His risk assessment changed as they moved around the room and as Old Man with Beard had left the room Old Bald Man became the highest risk.

* * *

Galston rounded up four coffee cups and filled the machine with water. His back was to the living room. He could hear Sandy speaking.

'Do ah need tae count it?' Sandy asked, looking direct at Ewan.

'Probably for the best,' he responded from the rear of the room.

Sandy looked at each of them standing there and smiled. He tested the combination on the second case and flipped it open. Then he turned back to them. 'Naw, it's ok, I trust you.'

Ewan and James shifted uncomfortably.

'Gal. Where's the fuckin coffee?' Sandy shouted through to the kitchen.

Tony looked towards the kitchen and then over at Ewan and James, his mind racing. There was something in Sandy's attitude, his voice. It was in that instant he realised this would never be over. No matter how well this morning went, he realised it. And less than a second later, he made a decision.

He raised his right arm.

* * *

It took Sandy six months to contact Galston after the night at the Market Bar. They disposed of Brian's body inside the foundations of the building works just a few meters from the exact spot where he had bludgeoned Billy to death. As they re-dug some founda-tions he glanced towards the Portakabin and images of his mushed face flashed through his head, he saw them and felt no emotion. It was if he was separate from it. He knew he was the person in the image kicking and battering the prone man to death but he felt nothing. Nothing at all. It was 4 am by the time they had finished with Brian and then without saying anything they went their separate ways. Sandy returned to the bar and compensated the owner with a mixture of cash and threats. He used his usual carrot-first approach and in this instance added the threat of a very heavy stick second. Most people, like Santa the barman, preferred the carrot. Donny knew better than to say anything and so Brian became just another missing person, most likely having moved back down south in search of gold and glory like so many other young men.

Galston was getting ready for a night out when the knock came at his door. He was stood in front of the mirror and stopped mid-comb. He had heard the knock but no one ever knocked at his door so for him it was an alien sound. He carefully placed the comb back into the glass next to the mirror holding a toothbrush and a razor blade and walked back through to his living/bedroom, listening intently. The knock came again, solid and insistent this time, there was no mistaking it. Galston buttoned up his paisley patterned shirt and opened the door.

Sandy stood there beaming.

'Galston! How ya doing, pal?' He walked inside without being asked, patting him on the shoulder as he brushed past. 'Long time? What ya up tae these days?' he said looking around the tiny bedsit.

Galston stood with his back to the open door watching him wander around his room. 'What dae you want, Sandy?' he asked but knew what he wanted, he had been waiting for this moment.

Sandy replaced the photo he had been studying and turned around. He was still smiling. 'I have a favour tae ask.'

Whenever Galston studies his life thus far, he always eventually comes back to this moment. It was that briefest of moments when he still felt he had a choice. Left or right? Up or down? Black or white? For him, this was the moment he still had some form of free will. He could still choose free of any persuasion. He could have told Sandy to get lost and gone out to meet Brenda. He could have killed Sandy there and then. These were choices. But he knew Sandy would come and had wanted him to come. The passage of time had altered the memory of that evening. The reality was he had no choice. Galston felt no remorse for Billy, Brian or James. He felt no elation either. He felt nothing about them nor what he did to them. The only thing he felt, the only constant at that moment in his life was the darkness within.

He calmly closed the door and sat down on the only chair in the room before speaking.

'Will ah get paid for this favour?' he asked.

* * *

Tosh breathed out and simultaneously increased the pressure on the trigger. As the rifle kicked back into his shoulder he saw Old Bald Man fly backwards over the wicker chair, a puff of red mist filling the void where he once was. The fact he had just killed a man did not enter his head. He kept the scope firmly trained on the conservatory, waiting for Old Man with Beard to reappear. Dust filled the air inside the room. His breathing remained controlled and he noticed absently that both Fat and Thin had thrown themselves to the floor. Tony had moved out of sight.

* * *

Micha heard the crack of gunfire about three metres away from where he stood and stopped dead still. He immediately noticed the barrel of the rifle sticking out through the gorse and long grass skirting the small copse. From where he was standing he could see his brother, running now, towards the building and some movement in the conservatory. He decided quickly that in any scenario a sniper wasn't a good thing so slowly and carefully removed the cosh from his pocket. All the time keeping his eyes fixed on the gun barrel. Taking a deep breath he took five steps, quickly covering the distance between him and where the rifle barrel was sticking out. As he walked he flicked the flexible metal weapon to its full length. Tosh heard the crack of the cosh extending and swivelled around. A second earlier he might have stood a chance. As it was, he turned just in time to see Micha bringing the dark metal weapon full force in a downward motion towards his skull.

* * *

Ewan and James had been walking slowly backwards since they had arrived in the room. It was an unconscious act driven by the burning need to leave the house. Sandy spoke to them, 'Do ah need tae count it?'

'Probably for the best.' Ewan had responded.

Sandy had shouted to Galston and it was then that all hell broke loose.

They watched Tony raise his right arm and for both of them it was so unusual they just stood there, their respective brains not linking the visual with the instructed action. They stood and watched as Sandy was thrown bodily backwards over the wicker chair. Red spattered the white wall behind him and plaster dust was thrown out from a jagged hole in the wall. It took them both more than a second to realise what had happened and throw themselves to the floor. As Ewan hit the floor he felt a hot burning sensation in his neck. He rolled onto his side and his hands reached for the source of the pain. The end of a five-inch wicker splinter stuck out from his neck. It felt warm and slick as blood pumped freely from the jugular vein it had punctured. Beside him James pressed his face into the carpet. The room fell silent.

Galston spun around at the sound and saw Sandy lying with his face pressed against the wall as if he was kissing it. His legs rested on the upturned wicker chair and he could see a dinner-plate-sized ragged hole in the back of his jumper. Blood splattered the wall above his body, Galston could see he was still moving. He glanced around the conservatory but couldn't see anyone and as he dropped down behind the kitchen counter he caught a glimpse of movement outside in the field. He squatted down, the coffee machine was still gurgling. His brain was trying to figure out what had just happened. Sandy had been shot that was clear, but by whom? Did the English guy have a gun? Was there someone in the field? He reached up and felt around for the kitchen knife block which he knew was there.

Tony walked over to Sandy, he was alive but wouldn't be for very long. He didn't even glance outside at the field. He knew where Tosh was and didn't need to confirm this. Sandy was proof enough of his existence. He saw Ewan and James lying down at the back so ignored them. He missed the pool of blood flowing from Ewan's neck and his near white complexion. He turned his attention towards the kitchen.

'Ok, so we have an issue,' he said loudly in Galston's direction.

'Well, *you* have an issue,' he corrected himself. 'Your boss is dead, we are armed and I'm guessing you want to leave here alive.'

There was no response.

'Here's my suggestion, you leave now, fuck off and don't return and we'll call it a day ok?'

Galston was sitting on the floor of the kitchen, his back against the drawers listening to this, he held two kitchen knives. His breathing was regular.

'Why the fuck should ah walk away?' he shouted back.

Tony laughed. 'Because if you don't you *will* die.'

Galston stood up, still holding the knives. He walked into the conservatory and faced Tony. 'Gae oan then ya cunt,' he spat at him, sweat was running down his flushed face. He could feel the familiar feeling take over his body, his muscles tensed as the anger increased. 'Gae oan then, fuckin shoot me. Fucking dae me over. Fuckin dae it NOW!' He was shouting and walking towards Tony who was walking backwards, drawing him into the middle of the conservatory.

Gerald softly opened the door to the house and walked in quietly listening to the shouting; Gun in hand, safety off.

Galston stopped dead centre in the conservatory and smiled at Tony. 'Ah know what you are doing, ya know?' he looked out at the field and waved, noticing a small hole in the double-glazed glass. 'So wha you waiting faer?' He glanced around the room and saw James and Ewan in the corner. Ewan was white, a large pool of blood surrounded him. 'Your mate there disnae look tae healthy,' he said.

Tony glanced over towards Ewan. He saw the puddle of blood and Ewan's deathly white complexion. He stepped towards him. At that exact moment Gerald stepped into the conservatory his gun raised.

Tony turned, saw Gerald, the gun and quickly moved around. He didn't think or consider his course of action, it was instinctive. Neutralise the most imminent threat and Gerald had just taken over from Galston as the most dangerous man in the room.

Micha watched this through the scope of the rifle and as he saw Tony move towards his brother he pulled the trigger.

The hollow pointed round was travelling at 2,000ft/second when it entered Tony's right bicep. It continued its journey and in less than one millionth of a second later entered his chest just under his armpit. It travelled through his chest cavity pushing a wave of destructive energy in front of it. By the time it had reached his heart the wave was about the size of a ping-pong ball, by the time it exited under his left armpit it was the size of baseball. As the round buried itself in the wall above Ewan and James he was already dead. His heart had been turned to mush and the left-hand side of his chest missing. Tony dropped like a stone on top of Ewan's close-to-lifeless body.

Galston didn't even try to understand what was happening. He took the opportunity of the distraction to firmly grip Gerald's extended gun hand, pointing it away from himself. He used his other hand to push him hard and fast into the hallway, taking himself and Gerald away from the killing zone of the conservatory as quickly as possible. A round buried itself into the wall to Galston's left, plaster exploded and covered them both. Gerald was off balance and Galston kept pushing him backwards until they crashed into the front door. The wood cracked under the impact. He kept one hand on his wrist and his forearm over his chest. With his other hand he quickly dragged the serrated kitchen knife hard across his neck, slicing it deep from left to right. He never questioned him or said a word. He just felt the knife dig deep and ripped it across. Gerald watched him and felt the warmth as his throat was opened up. He felt the smooth painted wooden door against his back, then greyness, then nothing.

Galston kept his grip on the gun until the man went limp. The house fell silent.

Micha dropped the rifle and started running towards the house. He had seen his brother being pushed out of the room and ran full speed to get to the house. As he ran he pulled his hand gun free. He skirted the hedge and ran straight for the front door his feet kicking up loose gravel.

Galston dropped Gerald's lifeless body and quickly skipped through each room on the ground floor checking; it was silent and empty. As he checked the master bedroom he saw Micha running fast towards the house so he darted back to the hall. Gerald's body was lying in a pool of blood blocking the door. He picked up his pistol, checked the safety was off and made sure there was a round in the chamber. He was calm, throughout the house there was death but he was calm, his heart rate barely higher than when he was in a deep sleep.

Micha reached the front door breathing heavily. He leaned against the wall next to the door and tried to slow his breathing and heart rate. He stood there and counted to sixty, slowly.

On the other side of the door Galston stood, waiting.

Micha gently pulled the handle down. The door was unlocked and he quietly pushed it open. There was something blocking it so he pushed a little harder, it moved, but only slightly.

Galston watched the door open, shunting Gerald's blood-soaked body. He stood behind it on the opposite side to the handle.

Micha pushed harder still and the door opened, he noticed a pair of feet on the thick carpet, he leaned in, gun first and then pushed his head through the door.

Galston raised the gun to head height and waited. He saw the gun come through the gap. He waited, his finger on the trigger.

Micha's head appeared and Galston squeezed the trigger. This was a lesson he had learned many years ago. Act first. Never hesitate, just do it. In a movie he would have said 'Freeze!' He might have disarmed the man and then perhaps restrained him. Galston did neither he just calmly pulled the trigger as soon as the opportunity presented itself and shot Micha in the right temple at point-blank range.

Death was instantaneous. Micha's head violently snapped away from him under the force, battering against the door frame. Blood, bone fragments and brain covered the far wall as half his head was ripped open. The neat scorched entry wound on the right side of his head contrasted starkly with the gaping wet flapping wound on the other side. He crumpled to the floor. Micha died three minutes after his brother and ended up on top of him, half in half out of the doorway.

Galston stood over them both for a second before returning to the conservatory.

Plaster dust still hung in the air but there was no movement in the house. He felt confident there was no risk from the field anymore. Tony lay draped over Ewan. James lay still in their pooled blood. He was alive but posed no threat. Galston kicked him. He didn't move. Sandy was moving but wouldn't be for long. Galston walked around the room and looked outside towards the field. The birds had gone.

He walked over to Sandy and turned him over. His face was white. He stared at him. He was conscious and looked back at Galston. Both men knew what was coming, even if he could have spoken Sandy didn't need to, he knew death was very close. Galston cradled his bosses head in his arms and spoke in a quiet, almost whispered voice.

'Ah know bout Tam.'

Sandy looked puzzled. He stared into Galston's eyes.

'Ah know it wis you,' Galston continued. 'I want you tae know a know before you gae. Ave always known it.'

Sandy tried to speak, there was panic in his eyes, but instead he just gargled blood which bubbled between his lips and ran down his chin. Galston watched him die and felt nothing.

He stood up dropping the lifeless body onto the floor and walked over to the two cases. He noticed James watching him from the corner of the room. Galston closed both cases and walked over to him.

'Clean yersel up, get the fuck away fae here and say nothing. Ah willnae come after you but if you ever think a doing anything. Anything, which might remotely have an effect oan me, ah will find ya and ah will fuckin kill you. You understanding me?'

James stared up at him and nodded.

'Good.'

Galston took the two cases and left the house stepping carefully over the two bodies at the front door. He placed the cases in the boot of his car and stood looking out over the gardens. There wasn't a sound. He was covered with blood, it had soaked into his shirt and trousers. His hands were white from plaster but he felt calm. The darkness had gone. He didn't know it then but he felt almost happy. He looked out over the rolling fields, lit a cigarette and let the events of the last twenty minutes run through his head. He didn't bother trying to analyse what had happened or how he felt about it, this would be for someone else to do if he could be bothered. He just stood there smoking and let the calm feeling wash over him in waves before dropping the cigarette, climbing into his car and pulling away.

* * *

James stood up as he heard the car leave and looked around the room. Sandy was lying where Galston had dropped him. He looked down at Tony and Ewan.

'Come on we need to get out of here,' he said as he walked into the middle of the room looking out towards the field.

There was no response, he turned and it was only then he noticed Ewan was not moving and his deathly white/grey colour. He rushed over dropping to his knees. It took some effort to move Tony's body. He had to use his shoulder and push with his legs to roll the dead weight off his friend. It made a sucking sound and then flopped over. Ewan looked up at him. His face normally red and flushed was devoid of any colour. His eyes flicked around, scanning James's face and the ceiling. James could see the wicker splinter sticking out of Ewan's neck and immediately knew there was little he could do. Ewan looked already dead apart from the eyes.

'Alright mate?' James said as he knelt next to his head in a puddle of blood; his jeans soaked up the bright red liquid.

Ewan's eyes focused on his friend. He tried to speak, his lips were moving but there was barely any sound.

'It's ok, Ewan, an ambulance is coming,' he lied. 'Just try to relax.'

Ewan's mouth formed a thin smile, 'Fushing liar,' he managed to get out, his whispered voice thin and raspy.

James put his hand on his forehead, 'Just rest.'

Ewan tried to move his body but nothing worked, he felt tired and sleepy. He knew he was dying, he wanted to believe James, wanted to believe that an ambulance would come and perform magic. He didn't want to die. He didn't want his life to end here. He lay there feeling baffled and angry. This wasn't how he had imagined it. It wasn't fair. Not now. Not like this. Most of all he felt guilty and didn't want that hanging over him.

'I'm sorry, James,' he whispered.

James never heard it. The whisper was barely audible. He just kept stroking his friend's head.

Ewan died.

* * *

Later that day Galston walked down Argyle Street, Glasgow heading west. There was a wind and he leaned slightly into it as he made steady progress past the new office buildings and executive flats. At the Anderston underground station he turned left and headed towards the river. There was no urgency in his walk, he wanted to walk but there was no reason and no real destination. When he reached the river he turned right and ambled towards some modern riverside flats. His footsteps flip-flopped parallel to the dark river, a body of water which had been a constant in his life. Whatever happened it was there regardless of the shit thrown into it, or the crap crossing over it. He made his way west slowly and watched as the planes took off from the airport further down the river. He had already made up his mind. He stared over the new-build flats and derelict land and felt no connection with anything he saw.

Galston stopped abruptly at a railing and looked across the river towards a modern shopping and entertainment complex. His mind was jumping from memory to memory, the landscape in front of him and around him changed with every image. Images came, flickered like a 9mm home movie and then left.

He stood there for ten minutes, leaning on the railing smoking as joggers, cyclists and couples passed him. They didn't even notice the grey-haired old man leaning on the railing. He was as much a part of the city as the river itself. His relevance had gone but like the last rusting remnants of the great shipyards which once lined the river he stubbornly persisted. Galston looked around, stood upright and flicked his cigarette into the water.

He then turned around and left.

Epilogue

The waves crashed hard against the coral in the distance.

From his vantage point halfway up the hill he saw the white breakers and a second later the sound reached his ears. An equatorial heat filled everything and he sat motionless, sweating. He was sitting on the porch of his small, modest house overlooking Coral Bay. Unlike most of the ramshackle houses on the island it was built of stone, one of the few built to withstand the annual tropical storms which would tear over the small Caribbean archipelago. He lived on the less popular South Island which was the smallest of the four habitable islands in the group and had no real tourist infrastructure to speak of. A small wooden jetty, a cluster of shops selling everything from light-bulbs to illegal distilled rum and Jimmy's dive school was pretty much the extent of its offerings. Access to the island was by boat to the much larger North Island and from there daily charter flights would fly to the US and further afield. He liked it this way, he liked the solitude. His house was filled with books, a small television, no telephone, no computer and he lived out a quiet existence, reading and thinking. He had no car and daily he would walk to the shop next to the jetty to buy provisions. This was his only exercise but combined with the heat his body had dropped ten kilograms since he arrived. He wore the same clothes every day, blue shorts and sandals. He couldn't remember the last time he wore anything on his upper body and the tight skin on his chest, face and legs had turned the colour of mahogany. The villagers were used to him, they ignored him as best they could, the strange man with a strange accent, he kept himself to himself and they appreciated this. In hushed tones they would warn their children not to go near the house on the hill, they would invent reasons why and the children would amplify this as they played. He was the Devil, he was a child molester, he would eat live fruit bats. One of them had actually seen it with their own eyes, and so on. In the three years he had quietly existed on the island he had become a myth. A bogeyman.

This suited Galston. He sat on the porch in the shade and watched the tourist boats bounce around the island, skirting the coral reef heading for the prime diving spots next to the smaller uninhabited islands. He lit a cigarette, ran his hand though his long grey beard and thought the thoughts of a man with very little on his mind.

Later that afternoon on the North Island a charter plane from Chicago touched down, its wheels squealing on the hot runway. It was a six-hour flight and when the seatbelt sign switched off the cabin was filled with people stretching and retrieving bags from the overhead lockers, all anxious to start their holiday. In seat 34C a young woman remained seated. She idly looked out over the heat-hazed tarmac as the cabin cleared. She shifted in her seat and smiled politely at the old couple who had shared her row as they left to start their golden wedding holiday. Eventually she stood and exited the plane, thanking the handsome young pilot as she stepped out onto the air-conditioned bridge. Within twenty minutes she was in a rusty taxi bumping its way down a pot-holed road heading for the docks and then onto a boat bound for the South Island.

Three years ago Sabine Weinstrom left the long-term psychiatric clinic in Interlaken with her memory intact. Over a six-month period it had returned, slowly and gradually at first and then in one big alarming gulp. Her childhood, her family, her job, her time in Heidelberg, Gustl, it all came back. Craig came back as well, her feelings for him, her love for him. She recognised now that she had fallen in love with him or at least that's what she remembered. Two and a half days and she had fallen in love with a man, was this possible? She questioned the memory but it was there, as strong as it was during their short time together.

Whenever she remembered him Galston was always close behind and with him came the other memories. They would jump into her mind, incomplete and random but she assumed her brain was protecting her from the full extent of what she had witnessed and survived. A winter wonderland of snow and pine trees. A clearing. Ice crystals floating in the freezing air. Blood, chunks of flesh, clothing. An arm. Galston grinning at her, grotesque and evil as he leaned over a bloody block, hacksaw in hand. It was with these memories that an unfamiliar darkness came.

When questioned she had purposely not mentioned the events of that night, her memory return was selective and the police reluctantly had to admit defeat. They apologised and told her should anything come back to call them.

Sabine travelled home to Dusseldorf and her parents.

It had taken her a long time to find him but when she did she would lie in bed and fantasise about the moment they would come face to face again. She dreamed of blood and as she walked off the South Island jetty that day her body was totally consumed with a dark murderous revenge.

After she purchased a claw hammer and some cable ties from the ramshackle hardware store she headed for the deserted pristine beach. She wasn't going to rush this. She wanted to savour every moment, she wanted to feel the elation she had long since dreamed about.

The sun beat down, there was a slight breeze washing over her and she padded barefoot over the loose white sand, enjoying the warm sensation sliding through her toes.

The darkness within was constant now. It was a feeling she had grown accustomed to over the years. It was part of her.

She sat down surveying the tropical paradise and thought of Craig.

Sabine Weinstrom was smiling.

Roundfire Books put simply, publish great stories. Whether it's literary or popular, a gentle tale or a pulsating thriller, the connecting theme in all Roundfire fiction titles is that once you pick them up you won't want to put them down.